"I want to see you."

Though the words could be taken as a re[...] His wants, she knew that they were heavier than that. Five typed words, one command sent via text message, and she had but a few minutes to comply completely. It did not matter that it was 4:07 a.m. or that she had been deeply asleep for at least 5 hours. She knew that keeping her phone under her pillow was necessary, as He could summon her at any moment and she had to be available, ready, and willing to do whatever was asked of her.

She groggily rolled off of the side of her bed, stumbling over her shoes then regaining her composure, and made her way to the bathroom. She splashed water on her face, removing remnants of her nightly facial mask, brushed her teeth, removed her scarf, and fluffed her hair a bit.

Staring briefly at her reflection, she thought, *This will have to do.* She turned on her computer and while it booted up, she went to the kitchen to grab a bottle of water. She glanced at the clock. 4:14 a.m. *Not bad.* She hurried to the couch and signed onto Skype. Within 30 seconds, her screen flashed with an incoming call.

"Good morning, beautiful girl..."

She smiled at His greeting, and put her headphones in. For some reason, listening to His voice through her earbuds made her feel closer to Him. She sat up straight, stared at His chest, and noticed that He wore no shirt. She could see the chest hair she'd fallen asleep against many times before. She felt familiar warmth slowly begin to spead across her skin.

"You may speak."

She continued to look at His chest, having not yet received permission to make eye contact.

"Good morning, Sir. It is an honor to be at your service. May I ask how you are?"

"You may."

"How are you, Sir? How was your day? Is there anything I can do for you at this time?"

"I am well. My day was long, rather exhausting. Look up..."

She raised her eyes without hesitation, meeting His sleepy but focused gaze.

"I'm being pulled so many ways at work. I know I can handle it, but some days... some days it is just too much. I must have clocked 15 hours today."

"Oh, Sir, I'm so sorry to hear that. I know you've been dealing with a lot at work lately and I hate that it is overwhelming you this way. How can I help you in this moment?"

"It would help if you followed my instructions and appeared on screen prepared," He began, a tinge of frustration in His voice.

"I've mentioned this before, so you're not unaware. Have you forgotten? Lost your rule book? What?"

She's felt the chills of disappointment prickle down her spine. In her sleepy disorientation, she'd forgotten to fully remove her clothing and attach her collar. The last time, she had gone to sleep with the collar on because He had demanded she do so. This time, it was beside her bed, in the drawer of her nightstand.

"Get it."

She scurried to her bedroom and withdrew her collar. She hastily fastened it to her neck and ran back to her computer.

"I don't remember telling you to put it on. Take it off... Now. You think you deserve to wear *my* collar right now? Never mind, don't answer that. I don't want to hear a word."

The bite of the last word forced her eyes to cast downward, shamed. Embarrassed, she removed the collar and held it in her hands. Her thumbs nervously rubbed over the ridges in the leather. She received the purple collar on her birthday, 9 months prior. After a year of training and service, she'd received her most coveted prize: His collar. She'd known better than to ask for it, but several times during any given week, she would catch herself fingering her neck longingly.

When out with her friends in The Life, she would often feel tinges of jealousy while looking at their beautiful collars. She would only hope that her submission pleased Him sufficiently and that He would, one day, bestow upon her His symbol of ownership. When He took her out for her birthday, during a walk in the park after dinner, He surprised her with the collar. He sat her down on a bench, stood behind her, and clasped it around her neck, whispering only, "You're mine." It was one of the best nights of her life and she cherished His gift and His appreciation of her. She never wanted to disappoint Him, but there were times, like this, when she faltered and made simple mistakes.

"I'm sorry, I--" she began.

"Don't be sorry. Do what I ask of you and prepare yourself accordingly when I summon you. It's rather simple, actually. Do as you're told. Look up..."

She looked up and met His eyes, this time seeing a smile. She didn't immediately understand where the smile came from, but she felt comforted. That was enough for her at the moment.

"Take off your clothes..."

This was not a new request and she knew very well what He wanted when He commanded it. He enjoyed her slow movements, never breaking eye contact... focused... deliberate... dancing on the bridge between coy sensuality and gratuitous sexuality.

She was wearing an ivory satin push-up bra and white boy shorts, so she didn't have much to remove. She reached behind her back and gingerly unhooked the latches of her bra. She then delicately hooked the index finger of her right hand under the left strap and guided it down her shoulder. She did the same for the other side, never breaking eye contact. She watched Him shift in His seat a few times, which she recognized as the onset of His arousal.

She was pleasing Him.

"Show me."

She fully removed the bra and cupped her breasts. They weren't overly large, but not small either. They were a full C cup, and He deemed them "perfect" for His taste. When He made this simple command, she knew He meant that she was to present them to Him, playfully and sensually, so she began massaging her breasts and rolling the nipples in between her thumbs and index fingers.

"Nice..."

She watched Him lean back in His chair and slowly place His hand atop His groin area. She could see slight twitches in His boxer-briefs, but dared not let her enjoyment of His new predicament show in her face because He could read her so well. She lifted her left breast towards her mouth, preparing to suck the nipple when He stopped her...

"Where's your toy? Go get it. Now."

She rushed to her bedroom again, opened the same drawer, and pulled out her lilac g-spot vibrator. She hurried back to her computer and looked at the screen. She saw that He had removed his boxer briefs and was holding Himself, slowly stroking back and forth, up and down. She knew what He needed. She sat back on her couch and lay back, spreading her legs.

"Push the button."

She turned on the vibrator and it began to buzz in her hands. She looked up at Him, meeting his eyes again.

"Sir, may I play with myself?"

"Yes. Do what I need you to do, what you need to do..."

Angling herself for a better view, she began to move the vibrator along the outer lines of her vagina. It slid in easily, as she was naturally well-lubricated. With her left hand, she spread the lips wider and with her right hand, she massaged herself with the lilac-colored device. With every movement, she slipped deeper into the moment and allowed herself more enjoyment of it. At least He'd given her permission to do so, this time. He told her to do what she needed to do and she proceeded to do just that.

She broke eye contact with Him when her own eyes began to roll back into her head. Her hips slowly began to gyrate to the rhythm her hand and toy had started. After a few minutes and at last three low groans from Him, she inserted the toy inside.

"Yes, baby girl. That's it. Show me. Good girl. Make my pussy cum for me. NOW!"

Hearing the urgency in His voice, she knew He was not far off from His own release. She knew He needed her to give Him the visual stimulation He needed to get over and release completely. Making Him cum was one of her greatest pleasures. To be able to serve Him in such a way, cater to His pleasure... she felt so lucky and honored to be the one He chose to be the source of His pleasure.

She widened her legs and pushed the toy deeper until it hit her spot. She knew it would be any second now. She moaned once, and then again, and finally a low, guttural raw sound came from her throat as she felt the wave of an intense orgasm take over her body. She felt her body jerk as her back arched and just then, her body released its juices and she squirted them all over her keyboard, some of it hitting the screen. She knew better than to be embarrassed by this, though, because He loved every drop that came from her.

She opened her eyes just in time to see Him making his final feverish strokes as He erupted into a handful of tissues he had. She hated to see His cum go to such waste, but what could she do?

"Did I please you, Sir?"

"Oh. Yes. Yes, baby girl. You were fantastic! You always are."

She beamed with pride, despite her temporary weariness.

"Good girl..."

"Thank you, Sir. I'm glad to be of service to you."

She lowered her head again, gathering her belongings. She'd clean it up tomorrow; she was too tired now.

"Nicole."

She looked up, having heard her birth name. She saw His hand extended, open palm, towards the camera.

"Yes, David?"

"I love you. So much..."

"And I adore you, my love."

"You are so fucking beautiful. I wish you could have come on this trip with me."

"I know, honey."

"I'll be home Friday."

"I can't wait."

"You may put your collar on. Sleep well with it until then."

"Ok, I will."

She blew Him a kiss and signed out of Skype. She padded back to her bed and stretched her limbs a bit to work out the kinks from their awkward positioning during their session. She lay down and heard the notification ring on her phone. She glanced at it and saw a text from Him.

"You're mine."

She typed the only response He needed and expected:

"Always."

This Is How It Works

Waking up before her alarm went off, Nicole lay in bed awake with her eyes closed. She spent a few minutes committing her dream to memory before she lost the details that could reveal some important revelation about her present and/or future. A believer in dreams, stars, mysticism and things of that nature, she did not take for granted what truths were being imparted upon her spirit by way of oft-overlooked occurrences, such as vivid dreams here and there.

In this particular dream, she was about seven months pregnant with twins, a male and female, and she was on bed rest because the male fetus showed early signs of potential cardiac issues. She remembered David being by her side in a hospital room, mulling over a decision related to the twins, but she could not remember exactly what it was. She focused a bit more... Nothing.

United 4679, 5:40 p.m., LGA. Black-and-white Donna Karan pinstripe pencil skirt, white silk Calvin Klein blouse. The peep toe pumps. Good luck today.

Her phone buzzed with a text from David. He was set to come home today from his business trip and she was excited to see Him. She knew that getting involved with a man who traveled a lot for business would be tricky and lead to many lonely nights, but she was supportive of His ambition and drive and happily accepted her role as being his primary support and biggest cheerleader.

Well, that was easy, she thought with a smile. She hated the time she wasted trying to figure out what to wear to important meetings at work. He knew this, of course, which is why He told her what to wear. He was also very particular about what He wanted to see when He arrived home. Rather than risk disappointment, Nicole consented early on to His dictation of her attire. He made His preference known, simply, and she fulfilled his wishes, completely.

She was presenting a proposal to the board of directors for the non-profit agency for which she was one of two Deputy CEOs. She wanted to start a new initiative that would create internship opportunities for current clients within the agency itself, since the poor economic climate limited work opportunities for the people with whom they worked. She'd done all of the necessary research and put together a 30-minutes presentation, complete with a slide show, short video and printed materials.

She felt both confident and nervous because this initiative was near and dear to her heart and she wanted to convince the board that it was worth the financial and human resource investment.

You'll do fine. Relax. You got this.

Her phone buzzed again… another text, right on time. He knew exactly how nervous she felt and how important today was in her career. He'd worked it out so that He could get an earlier flight and come back to be there for her when her work day was done. She loved that about Him, the effort He made to be supportive of her.

Nicole showered and dressed, then did her hair and make-up. Conservative, mostly, with enough subtle sex appeal to grab the attention of those who might be interested. One of the things she'd become better at during the time she'd been involved with David was embracing her femininity, her sensuality, and using it to her advantage when necessary. A little employment of feminine wiles never hurt anyone, she would come to discover.

With that in mind, she unbuttoned the top button of her blouse, exposing her "work collar". She had a few collars, a variety to choose from in whatever environment or circumstance she found herself in. He made sure of that. For work, she wore a simple sterling silver herringbone necklace with a platinum heart charm. Engraved into the back of the charm was one word: *Mine*. Each piece given to her by Him made clear that she belonged to Him… and she reveled in that.

After one last glance into the mirror, and one quick caress of the heart charm, Nicole took a deep breath, grabbed her valise and other presentation items, and left for work.

....

5:34 p.m.

Nicole impatiently tapped her fingers on the steering wheel of her Chevy Malibu. A nervous tick of hers, she found that the brevity with which she tapped her fingers directly correlated to the trouble she anticipated she'd find herself in.

She was late.

Though He indicated that His flight landed at 5:40 p.m., she knew that arriving at least 30 minutes ahead of schedule was what He considered her being on time. Occasionally, flights arrived early and He hated having to wait in crowded airports. Of course today, of all days, is the one where His flight landed at 5:22 p.m. and she was nowhere near the airport.

Where are you??

When she received that text message, Nicole knew she was in trouble. If she knew anything, she knew He never wanted to have to question where she was; He was to be in the know at all times. When she received the text alert that His flight had landed, and she was at least 10 minutes away, she knew what was in store for her. She prepared herself for the chastisement, swallowed every urge to refute and explain, and accepted her shortcoming for what it was- a disappointment to Him. She had another disappointment to explain, the reaction to which she feared even more.

She bombed her presentation.

From the slideshow she spent weeks working on not working properly, to her administrative assistant having not brought paper copies, to her spilling her coffee on poster charts she'd paid a great deal for, to one of the board members falling asleep, Nicole felt like completely failed at one of the most important presentations of her career.

She tried to salvage what she could and rely on her outstanding verbal skills, and most of the members seemed to be supportive, but she didn't feel that she was able sell the idea beyond any doubt or question as she'd intended. She braved a smile through handshakes and nods, but walked away with the sinking feeling that she'd failed and her project would not receive the approval she sought.

For the rest of the day, she found herself lost in her own mind, drowning in doubts of her abilities. She dared not express them to Him because He hated when she got like this. She knew, though, that the first thing He would inquire about upon being greeted at the airport would be the presentation. As if the disappointment she had in herself wasn't enough

5:57 p.m.

"You're late. You may speak."

"I know. I'm sorry, Sir..."

"Explain yourself."

"My day didn't go so well."

"And that takes priority over your obligation to your service and responsibilities?"

"Of course not!"

"Watch your tone…"

"I'm sorry, Sir."

"Let's go"

David began walking, heading towards the parking lot leaving his suitcase where it stood. Nicole knew He meant for her to bring it and follow behind Him. *And so it begins*, she thought to herself. This was her penance for being late and taking an agitated tone with Him. She grabbed his suitcase and followed behind Him, head down. It was an embarrassment for her to carry His bag, as He would never have His woman, whom he cherished, carry His bags.

David stopped walking and Nicole continued, knowing she had to guide Him to where the car was parked. Walking in front of Him was something she was never completely comfortable with, but she figured this was part of her penance too. His leading was something she craved, especially after periods when He'd been away on business and she spent several days without His physical guidance and leadership. She quickened her pace, hoping He would follow suit. Instead, He continued to walk with slow, measured steps, each one more deliberate than the last… each tap of the heels on his chocolate brown Kenneth Cole loafers heightening her anxiety.

When they arrived at the car, He opened her door and she slid inside. He put His suitcase in the trunk, entered the driver's side and turned the key in the ignition.

"How did your presentation go?"

She knew this question was coming and no matter how many ways she considered presenting the truth to Him, she knew she would not be able to avoid telling it. She remained quiet, breathing deeply, a mixture of embarrassment, disappointment, anger, frustration, and the overwhelming desire to please Him stirring inside of her. Tears began to form behind her now-closed eyelids. She sniffed them back.

"Nicole…"

David turned to look at her and she felt His gaze burning through her. He knew her, so well. When they first met, they were both amazed by how easily and quickly they fell in close with each other. They were comfortable, almost immediately, and became close friends rather quickly. She seemed to see Him plainly, for who He was, in ways most people in his life, even life-long friends seemed to overlook. He recognized, in her, a support system, a friend, a confidant, a cheerleader, and later, a fantastic lover. She felt that He was genuinely interested in who she was, the woman behind the mask, and He made it clear that He had no intention of letting her go, no matter how their relationship developed.

Things were intense for them both from the very beginning. They were each recently coming out of romantic situations, both scared to rush into new ones. They took much-needed time getting to know each other, enjoying each other's company and reveling in the newness and simplicity of dating. From the beginning, she recognized the natural Dominance in Him. She was drawn to it, compelled to serve and please Him, beyond anything that even made sense that early; He was her One.

Before her submission informed her of this fact and before His Dominance claimed her as His to own, they could not deny it. He'd been unsure of Himself, at least in terms of how to display His Dominance with her; this was somewhat new to Him. He asked her to help Him learn, to guide Him so that He could grow to be what she needed in a Dom. She was more than happy to do so and, in the beginning, she would often drop hints here and there. She had more experience in "The Life" than He did, but He never seemed intimidated by that. She was never overbearing or chastising. She gently guided Him with subtlety He appreciated.

The more time they spent, either in person, online, or via phone, the more comfortable He grew in His Dominance, she in her submission, and they grew together. Their love for each other grew, slowly, surely, intentionally, and purposefully. He would eventually take over and she no longer needed to tell Him what she needed and craved; He knew. David came to know and fully understand Nicole's needs like the back of His own hand and was intrinsically tuned into her desires.

Now, as they sat in the car cloaked in excruciatingly loud silence, intense electricity began to form between them. Still, she said nothing. She couldn't. In the next second, His left hand was clasped firmly around her throat, forcing her face upwards. His lips were less than an inch away from her left ear and she could feel the warmth of his breath against her eardrum.

"Answer me."

She opened her mouth, but no words came out. She responded, just not verbally. As she felt her panties dampen, she closed her eyes and for the first time that day, felt herself relax a bit. He was home.

He turned her face towards His and she opened her eyes. He searched her face for answers and she read in His eyes that He was beginning to understand what was wrong with her. His face softened and His hand released its grip of her throat. She leaned back and fastened her seatbelt as he fastened his own, checked the rearview mirror, and put the car in reverse. He paused, slightly.

"Crop or cane?"

"Cane."

"Ok. Let's go home."

6:58 p.m.

She'd been on her knees for fifteen minutes. When they arrived at home, she immediately removed her clothing, put on her collar, and took her place on her knees on the service pillow He'd had made for her. When she was being disciplined or punished, no pillows were allowed and she had to deal with the discomfort of their hardwood floors.

This time was different, though. This scene was for release. David had the pillow custom made for her, purple satin case with the word "HIS" sewn into it in cursive. She waited for Him while He showered and used the time on her knees to clear her mind and spirit as much as possible. She had to prepare to receive Him and what was to come.

She was so intensely into her meditation that she didn't hear Him walk up behind her. She was startled when she felt her head jerked back by a hand wrapped in her hair.

"I'll ask again. How did your presentation go?"

She said nothing, still feeling paralyzed by embarrassment. Her lips parted slightly, but the words didn't come. The warm sting of the bamboo cane as He brought it down across the right cheek of her buttocks was a welcomed distraction. Then the second... and the third... and then the fourth.

She felt the heat spread across her skin as he pulled her head back further. Her eyes remained closed and unconsciously licked her lips. She felt the pluck of His fingertips across her lips.

"Don't get too comfortable, Star. You are a nasty girl, indeed, but this isn't the time for that. Focus."

Star was her "sub" name, the name He'd given to her when He claimed her as His. He had once said that she shone brilliantly as the brightest reflection of His light, so "Star" was the perfect name for her.

"I asked you a question. Twice. With no answer, yet. Have you forgotten how this works?"

She shook her head as best she could, given the tight grip He had on her hair.

"This is how it works: I ask, you answer. You don't answer, I make your skin burn. Do you understand? Speak."

She nodded her head in response.

"I said 'Speak'!"

For emphasis, He drew the hand wielding the bamboo cane further back and brought it down harder again the same surface area He had just reddened. She flinched this time, quite visibly. She was beginning to feel the painful side of it.

She remained silent. He drew back and smacked her again. Again, she flinched, this time falling forward a bit, as far as she could go with His other hand grabbing her hair. He could tell the pain was getting to her, but she was holding something stronger back.

"Talk to me, Star. Tell me what happened. Speak now!"

Another whack, this time on the left cheek. He took care not to overdo it and do anything that could lead to permanent tissue damage. He knew that alternating spots to strike was important, and would elicit different responses. He also knew that she was far more sensitive on the left side, which He was reminded of when she let out a painful yelp.

"I blew the presentation!"

"What do you mean?" He asked as he pulled her, by hair, back to a tall kneeling position. When she didn't speak immediately, He struck her on the left cheek again.

"What. Do. You. Mean??"

Each word was accompanied by another strike of the cane. Two strikes on the upper portion of her cheek, two on the lower. She whimpered, falling forward again. This time He let her hair go and let her fall forward. She sniffed back tears again, as she did in the car.

"Oh no you don't..."

He struck her again, this time on the backs of her upper thighs. Ten cane strikes, even tempo, consistent force, different parts of her thighs. This was her weakest area. She usually didn't last very long when He focused there. The tears began to flow freely. She didn't lift her face to him. She began rocking back and forth crying harder with every rocking movement.

"Tell me, Star. Tell me what happened that was so bad."

She stopped rocking and the words poured forth. She told Him everything about the mishaps of the presentation and how she felt like a complete failure. He stood quietly, cane still in hand, and listened intently. He didn't caress her or even touch her with His hands at all. He let her have this moment, this release. He stood firm in front of her, which was all she needed in that moment. She cried through her recount, letting go of the tears she'd been holding back the entire day.

At the end, she fell forward, placing her forehead on the tips of His now bare feet.

"I'm so sorry, Sir. I'm sorry I let you down. I'm sorry I failed you. I'm sorry I failed myself. You believe so much in me. You helped me with this for weeks. You've shown me so much care and support...and I failed. Forgive me, please!"

Teardrops landed on His feet and rather than brush them away, she rubbed them in. He loved when she washed His feet with her tearful releases.

"You did not fail me. You did not fail yourself"

"Yes I did!! Yes I did!!"

"Are you disputing me and my assessment? Is that what is happening right now?"

"No, of course not, Sir. I'm sorry. I... I'm just struggling with this."

"Let it go, Star."

"It's not that easy."

"I said... Trust in me and Let. It. Go. Now!"

With that last command, He grabbed her by her arms and pulled her up off of her knees. They were now standing face-to-face, almost eye-to-eye. He shook her shoulders a bit.

"You have to let it go. You did the best you could. You encountered a few mishaps, but it happens to the best of us."

She looked down into His eyes. She couldn't seem to bring herself to accept what He was saying as truth. He lifted her chin up with His index finger. He leaned closer and kissed her, softly at first, then increasingly deeper as He sought to convey His love and appreciation for her and her intelligence and skills. She felt herself relax and melt into His arms. He caught her. He always catches her.

He gently led her to their bedroom and guided her to lie on their bed. She couldn't lie on her back, as her skin was still on fire, so she lay on her stomach. He retreated to the bathroom and retrieved the skin cream she liked, the one that soothed her best after a scene like this. He gently applied the cream to the areas He could see were in need of tender care. When He was done, He lay in bed next to her, sitting up on their pillows.

"Service me."

She moved towards Him, taking Him into her mouth. This was her favorite way to pleasure Him and He thoroughly enjoyed the warmth of her mouth and the skilled ways in which she almost devoured him. He could feel her throat massaging His tip, her tongue lavishing attention on His shaft, and he leaned His head back closing His eyes.

"I'm going to cum this way tonight, so don't you dare stop."

She had endurance, so this command was no issue for her. She continued to "service" Him for the next 30 minutes or so. She could feel Him reaching His end.

"God, baby, I've missed this. You are the fucking best, Nicole. Shit. Ahhhh fuck... FUCK!!"

He exploded in her mouth, deep into her throat, grabbing her head and forcing Himself as far down her throat as He could go. He heard her gag a bit, but knew she could handle it; this was her best skill. He allowed her a moment to swallow Him and clean Him up with her tongue.

"Did I please you?"

"Oh, fuck yes. Nicole, I can't ever give this shit up. Your mouth is a fucking goldmine!"

She smiled, sweetly, having received the praise she needed for the evening. He slid down further under the sheets and pulled her close and tightly to Him. He kissed her on her forehead.

"You are one of the smartest people I've ever encountered in my entire life. You're beautiful, inside and out. There will be other opportunities to present your idea and garner support. All is not lost. You didn't fail me. You didn't fail yourself."

He kissed her forehead again.

"Get some rest. You're going to need it for the morning."

She knew that meant He was going to fuck her silly when they woke up and she giggled to herself. She closed her eyes and prepared to fall asleep, wrapped up in His protective, reassuring embrace.

"I love you, baby girl. You're my most valued prize"

"I love you, too, David. Glad you're home..."

SAPPHIRE

"We're going to play this weekend, Star."

David whispered into her ear eight minutes before her alarm went off. Nicole smiled, as her eyes closed, and backed herself closer to Him, aligning the roundness of her bottom with the now-pulsing hardness of His obvious desire. In that moment, they were separate entities. In the next, they were one, as He spread her cheeks and entered her, claimed her for the day.

Gasping, she opened her eyes and stared straight ahead at the lamp on the nightstand, still lying on her left side. He grabbed her right leg, lifting it and drawing it back over His thigh and pushed deeper into her. An errant moan escaped her lips and was immediately followed by a stinging smack to her thigh, then His strong hand around her throat.

"Shut. The. Fuck. Up."

David and Nicole awoke in a foreign bed together at a hotel paid for by her company. She had a conference to attend for three days and two nights and David joined her for the second night, arriving from California the day before. They both knew He shouldn't have been there, especially since a colleague she never got along with was in the next suite, but they also didn't care much because it had been almost two weeks since they had seen each other. Still, she couldn't be as loud as she normally was.

"I swear, on everything, I'll never stop being impressed by how fucking good you take this dick. Shit. God, woman..."

He quickened the pace and deepened the penetration. With every stroke, she seemed to get wetter, which only made Him fuck her more furiously. He pushed her onto her stomach, pushed her legs together and straddled her cheeks. He spread her cheeks wide so He could watch Himself go in and out of her. *Mine,* He thought to Himself.

After several minutes in this, her favorite position, He grabbed her neck again, this time turning her face so she was face down into the pillows. Nicole stretched her arms out in both directions and grabbed the sheets, clenching them. It was coming.

"Breathe."

She drew in a deep breath just in time. Within seconds a pillow descended onto her face and she was eclipsed in white. One, two, three, five, ten, twelve of the slowest seconds passed as she felt herself falling deeper into sub-space, her mental, physical, spiritual, and emotional place of peace and freedom, embracing her temporary loss of breath and reveling in the strength and love He provided. Fifteen, eighteen, twenty seconds and assaults on her pussy later, she knew she was about to release. She let go of the sheets, her sign to Him that she was ready. As if that ever mattered...much. She wanted to cum and she was seeking permission to do so.

"Nah."

He removed the pillow from her face, pinched her cheek, and she drew in a deep, gasping breath, eyelids fluttering as she abruptly came back to her senses.

"You have a speech to give in an hour," He said with a laugh. "Get up and go brush your teeth, then come back here."

She fought the urge to pout. She quickly got out of bed and hastened to the bathroom, doing as instructed. A few minutes later, she came back to where He sat on the side of the bed stroking Himself, still hard and thick as He was moments prior.

"Open up."

She got on her knees and opened her mouth wide and He immediately shoved Himself down her throat. After a few quick deep strokes, He eased back and unleashed in her mouth. A little bit spilled out of the side and He quickly pushed it back in.

"Swallow."

She swallowed every drop of Him and licked her lips. She started to get up to go and gargle one more time. Of course, He knew her intention and grabbed her arm.

"Nope. Not today," He said with a wink. "It'll be like we're giving the speech together." David laughed at His corny humor and Nicole shook her head. She didn't gargle, though. She knew better.

"Speak."

"Sadist."

"Yeah, well..." He laughed again.

"We're playing this weekend, Sir?"

"Yes. We've both been busting our asses these past couple of weeks. We deserve a break, don't you think?"

"Agreed. One hundred percent. Where are we going?"

"Sapphire, of course."

"Of course."

"Have I become predictable?" He turned to her and raised an eyebrow.

"Not at all. I just know you love that spot."

"And you don't?"

"Well, I didn't say all of that. You know I do."

"Alright, then. Stop acting like you aren't excited, nasty ass," He chided with a laugh.

"What should I we–"

"The red-and-black striped cocktail dress. Red heels. Scene collar. I packed them in my bag before I left."

"So you planned this already? You were going to surprise me, Sir?" she asked with a smile and cheerful, giddy clap.

"All these questions," He began, shaking His head. "Get dressed. You have work to do and so do I." He turned away from her and walked towards the desk to turn on His laptop.

"Fix your face, baby girl."

He said that just as she was scrunching her nose at Him behind His back. Busted. She got up and went to the bathroom to take a shower and go over the key points of her speech. She'd ironed their clothing the night before, so she didn't have to worry about that. With a few deep breaths, she prepared to take on the final day of the conference without being distracted by the sperm swimming in her teeth.

****

Sapphire was an out-of-the way social club for "adult" party-goers. It was the only spot in a 200-mile radius that combined a Dungeon and a Swing Club in one. Usually, swing clubs focused primarily on dancing and sex, often in private rooms, one of which might have a BDSM theme to it. Most dungeons didn't allow people to engage in sexual activity and, more specifically, didn't allow fluid exchanges.

Sapphire was the one place people who were both into BDSM and the Swinging lifestyle could come and enjoy themselves in a night of complete hedonistic indulgence. David and Nicole purchased a membership six months prior and had gone three times since. Each time, they discovered something or someone new and always left feeling closer to each other; it was a great enhancement to both their relationship and their sex life.

There was a BDSM convention in town, and though David was unable to register them for the workshops and panels, He was able to get passes for entry that night since the convention organizers rented the location out for their private use. Literally hundreds of people in The Life had convened for the weekend and at least half were expected to be at Sapphire that night. At least they knew that there would be people there who were more into playing than just watching, which is the focus of many of the people who normally go to Sapphire.

The first time David and Nicole went, they agreed they wouldn't "play" with others and keep to themselves, which they did. Of course, the environment was arousing and He required servicing from her, but that didn't really count...or at least that's what they rationalized at the time. The second time, He let her play with a woman who was part of another couple while He and the woman's husband watched. The third time, she was actually on punishment, so He used various devices and tools to give her a strong lesson in disobedience that left her almost unable to stand on her own. He then made her lie on a bed and watch Him give another woman the fucking she would have received, were she not such a petulant, disobedient brat.

Lesson learned.

This time was a bit different, as they both knew quite a few of the people in attendance. Both David and Nicole were active on a social media site for people in The Life, she more than Him, but they both had profiles. They'd met other people at previous events and gatherings and were embraced by their peers as a D/s couple in The Life.

While in line to get into the club, Nicole ran into one of her girlfriends, Aaliyah, who came down with her Master for the convention. She curtsied in deference to Aaliyah's Master, out of respect, as did Aaliyah to David. They chatted a bit, as sub sisters do, catching up on what was going on in and out of The Life, while their Sirs talked a bit. It was a reunion of sorts, as both David's and Nicole's schedule didn't allow them free time to be as involved in Lifestyle events as others. They did what they could, when they could.

The music in the club was bumping heavy bass and there was already a large crowd on the dance floor. People were crowding around the bar, chatting, laughing, catching up it seemed. People were dressed in everything from scant club attire to sexy fetish gear. There was a plethora of leather and lace, black, red, purple everywhere. It was the type of sexy environment Nicole loved and from which she drew her most sensual energy. She felt herself becoming charged by the electricity in the room already. David's hand made it to the small of Nicole's back and grabbed a bit of the material on her dress, a subtle possessive gesture that she immediately recognized. She didn't ask what prompted it, but she became more mindful of her behavior and her representation of Him and their union.

"Sir, would you like a drink?"

"Not yet, Star. I do have to use the restroom though."

She began to walk towards the restroom to escort Him, but He stopped her. He pulled out His wallet and handed her a $20 bill.

"Get yourself a drink, baby girl. I'll be right back. I expect you'll conduct yourself accordingly," He said with a smile.

"Of course, Sir," returning His smile in kind.

He kissed her forehead and as He walked off, she turned around and placed an order at the bar. Vodka and cranberry was the drink of the night, she decided. The deep red would match her outfit sexily. While she waited for her drink, her hand went to her collar which felt a bit tighter than usual. She didn't dare loosen it; He placed it as tight as He wanted it to be this evening. She tugged at it a bit, to adjust it a bit more comfortably.

"Maybe it shouldn't be there. Ever think of it that way?" said a voice as dark as a cave and as smooth as the Devil.

Nicole dropped her hand, lifted her head up and stared into the darkest eyes she'd ever known. They belonged to a 6'5" ex-professional football player with cinnamon skin, broad shoulders, legs as thick as tree trunks, and waist-length, neatly-groomed dreadlocks: Marcus.

"Shit."

Nicole turned away from him and focused on the bartender making her drink.

"So you're not happy to see me? Well, I'm happy to see you. You look good enough to eat, Luna."

"Do not call me that."

"I'll call you whatever I want and you will respond. Isn't that right?"

"No."

"And yet, you just did. I trained you so well…" he said with a smirk. He took out a $10 bill and handed it to the bartender. "Her drink is on me," he said.

"I can pay for it myself, Marcus."

"What did you call me?"

Nicole glared at him. She wanted nothing more than to punch him in his mouth, but she knew better than to ever disrespect David in such a way.

"Oh, I see. You've not had any good direction in your life in quite some time, so you're acting like any common, disrespectful girl out here. I see how you are. At least you are still fine as hell. You been working out? You've lost a lot of weight. You must not be eating good like you used to."

"Don't speak of my Sir in that way."

"Your 'Sir'?" Marcus laughed loudly, mockingly. "Oh, please. Is that why you can pay for your drink yourself? No real man would let his girl pay for her own drinks. Come now, let me buy you a drink and let's catch up. It's been a while, Luna."

"My name is Star."

Marcus raised the sleeve on his shirt and revealed a tattoo of a Moon with a feminine face, turning towards her. "Luna."

"Marcus… leave me alone," she said, with the slightest hint of pleading.

"No, Nicole."

"I think the lady asked you to leave her alone," David interjected, having walking up behind Marcus silently.

Marcus turned around, facing David with a dismissive smirk. David looked past Marcus and caught Nicole's eyes. The hint of fear in her eyes flipped a switch in Him.

"And you are?" Marcus asked David.

Marcus was taller than David, and he looked down towards Him with annoyance, not knowing how He and Nicole were connected. David walked around Marcus to stand in front of Nicole. He pushed her behind Him, His right arm extended behind Him and resting on her hip. He grabbed Nicole's drink from the bar with His left hand and took a slow sip. After placing the glass back down on the bar, returned Marcus' mocking stare with His own declarative one.

"I am the Man that will snap your neck where you stand if you even fix your mouth to utter another word to My Bitch again."

4:46 p.m.

Nicole glanced at the clock on her computer, nervously anticipating the end of her work day. She originally planned to take a 5:30 p.m. conference call, but rescheduled it when he told her that he needed her home by 6:00 p.m. He said that he had something "special" planned for her. The important call had taken two weeks to arrange, as it included several directors from agencies across the Northeast. She hated having to reschedule, but she knew better than to tell him "No" once he made it clear that he had made plans.

She wasn't exactly sure how things had gotten to this point, but she did the best she could give their dynamic. She worked it out so that the call would take place in the morning and now sat at her desk tapping her fingers, working out a plan. She could leave early, but her nerves were rattled and she was delaying the inevitable. She'd learned the hard was that with him, "special" didn't always mean "good". She didn't allow herself to fall into memories of not-so-great times, so she turned her attention back to work.

She finished sending off the emails she needed to get out in preparation for the conference call and, after another fifteen minutes or so, began to gather her belongings. After a quick trip to the restroom to freshen up, she headed to her car and made her way home. She popped in a Stevie Wonder compilation CD she made filled with her favorite love songs of his. She began to hum along to "Joy Inside My Tears". *You, you, you... made like history...you brought the joy inside my tears...* Seemed like she'd had more tears than joy lately, but...that happens in relationships, she guessed.

Traffic was unusually light this evening and she said a silent prayer of appreciation because being late was not even remotely an option. Pulling off of the expressway at the exit that would take her to her neighborhood, she began to feel sick to her stomach. Saying a silent prayer for mercy, she locked up her car in the garage and headed to their home.

5:58 p.m.

As she got off of the elevator, Nicole could hear the velvety tone of Luther Vandross's sultry voice wafting through the hallway coming from their apartment. She couldn't help but smile because she knew that meant he was "in the mood". She shook her head at her own worry, exhaled the deep breath she only now realized she was holding, and walked towards the door.

As she got closer, she smelled chicken frying. *He is cooking? What on earth?* She knew he had something "special" planned, indeed. If he cooked once a month it was excessive. The kitchen was certainly her domain and that is how he expected it to be, so whenever he cooked, she became suspicious. *What does he want now?* She tried to ignore the concerns developing in her head and keep an open mind. *You never know...*

She walked into the apartment greeted by a stronger aroma of chicken frying and a freshly-baked sweet potato pie, both his specialties. She remembered how he brought her a homemade sweet potato pie on their second date, which was rather impressive because it actually tasted delicious. As she took off her coat, she could hear him making his way towards her. She looked up and saw that smile, the smile that made her weak still, years later. His parents spent good money on that smile, as he often joked, so he made it his business to flash his perfect set of teeth whenever possible. She loved seeing it now; it felt comfortably reassuring.

He walked towards her, reaching in to wrap his arms around her waist and bury his face in her neck. As he inhaled her scent, she laced her arms around his neck, gently biting his ear. She felt his response as he pulled her closer against his lower body.

"See, you trying to get things started already," he chided.

"Well, Sir, you're the one in here cooking my favorite foods and playing "big" Luther, and you said you had something special planned for me, so..." she reminded him.

"Mmmhmmm," he moaned into her neck. "I absolutely do. But first, we eat! Go undress while I finish cooking and I'll meet you in the dining room," he said with a kiss on her cheek and a light smack on her buttocks. She jumped, giggling, and made her way to their bedroom.

While undressing, she thought about how this was a nice change for them. Things had been rough recently and Nicole had so many conflicting thoughts and feelings running through her mind, heart, and spirit. There were more times than not when she felt like he didn't have her best interests in mind or that he was being overly demanding. Sometimes, the punishments were harsher and hurt more than they should have, and they were for the slightest infractions.

Yes, he was a sadist and she knew this, but something was different lately. She was beginning to feel like maybe he'd established some impossible standard for her that she could never meet or when she came close, he raised it even higher. Nothing she did seemed to satisfy him anymore. In the beginning, he lavished her with regular praise and prizes for her diligent service. These days, he barely uttered "Thank you" or "Good girl" when she provided him with good service, and it left her questioning herself and whether or not she was cut out to be a good submissive. She just wanted him to be happy with her.

This evening, however, he seemed to be in a different place, reminiscent of their earlier days. She couldn't stop smiling if she wanted to; this was what she needed.

"Luna?!" he called out, summoning her.

"Coming, Sir!!" she responded, making her way to the dining room, having fully disrobed of her work clothes.

Rule #4: You will wear no clothing while in this house unless it's that time of the month. You can wear panties then. You may also wear an apron when cooking.

"Do you need help with anything, Sir?"

"Not at all. I got you," he said with a wink. "Baby, I know you've been working so hard lately and I know I haven't been the most attentive. It's just that the whole Junior situation has had me completely stressed out, yanno?"

She nodded, understanding the weight he must be bearing since his older brother, Damon Jr., was arrested for armed robbery earlier that month. His bail was set higher than their family could afford to post, so his brother was set to remain in jail until his trial began. No date was set yet, so their family was anxiously awaiting more information and trying to hold everything together in the interim.

"Just let me take care of you again, for once," he said, looking tenderly into her eyes. She sympathetically met his gaze and smiled. She reached and caressed his arm.

"I appreciate it, Sir, thank you," she said before digging into her food.

They enjoyed great conversation while eating. She updated him on some of her projects at work and he updated her about the progress with Junior, as well as some new contracts he'd secured. He owned a small construction business which was picking up more business in recent months. His guys did amazing work and word of mouth was extremely positive, so he was beginning to reap the rewards of that with securing several new contracts that would carry him through the next 18 months at least.

When they first met, he was still struggling with simply breaking even, but she recognized his potential and was drawn to his ambition and his drive. She'd given him a small loan early on, against her usual judgment and practice, but she had faith in him. He paid it back with interest within a year and he often remarked on how essential she'd been to his business developing into what it was now. She was quite proud of him, as he was of her.

"It's funny you mention Lisa being pregnant..." he began. He put his fork down and looked across the table into her eyes again, his own growing darker. She knew this look, had seen it many times over the years. He was hungry, for her, and was about to feast.

"Stand up."

Nicole stood up immediately. His voice changed. She knew where they were, in this moment.

"Come here."

She walked over to where he sat still in his chair. He backed it up a bit and turned his body so that he was facing her. He unbuckled his belt and unzipped his pants, his arousal making its presence well known.

"Down."

She immediately fell to her knees and bowed her head. He first trailed his finger along her temple, and then wove his finger into her hair, grabbing a tight handful when his hand reached the back. He jerked her head up and stared down at her.

"Open up."

She opened her mouth and he swiftly pulled her head towards him until he was nestled deeply in her throat and her lips grazed his freshly shaved pubic area. He gently guided her head up and down along his shaft, moaning with pleasure as her warm mouth surrounded him. He placed his other hand in her hair and quickened the pace. He then stood up, never breaking their connection, and began to move his hips back and forth, trying to get as deep into her as he could.

He looked down and saw that her eyes were squeezed shut and tears were beginning to fall. He smiled, delighted, and held her face against him. He could feel her gagging and knew she was on the brink of regurgitation...and it felt heavenly. Her mascara began to run and he thought he would explode right then and there. Instead, he pulled her head back and simply stared down at her, panting and gasping for breath.

"Are... you done ...with my throat... Sir?" she eked out. "Did I... please you?"

"Of course, my Luna. You're amazing, simply amazing," he responded, caressing her face.

He pulled her up to her feet and kissed her deeply. He pulled her body to his and she began to unbutton his shirt. She felt her own desire peaking and she needed to have him inside of her. Before she could undo the fourth button, he hoisted her up and tossed her over his shoulder. She loved when he did that; it made her feel delicate and protected by a strong man. His long strides to the bedroom carried them both swiftly to their king-sized bed. In one smooth move, he placed her on the bed, spread her legs, and possessively entered her dripping wetness. She was more than ready to receive him and she wrapped her legs around his waist locking him inside of her.

He positioned himself above her, his long muscular arms bracing him above her head. He leaned on his forearms for support and he plowed into her. She met every stroke, thrusting her hips to meet his, keeping the beat to their perfect rhythm. Within minutes he had her on the brink of orgasm. He then grabbed her throat with his right hand. She arched her neck back and he clasped his grip tighter around her throat. She began to shake as her orgasm consumed her, and her eyes rolled into the back of her head. He leaned deeper into her, pushing her legs back even more, trying his best to rearrange her internal organs if at all possible. He began to get frenzied. He tossed his head back, his shoulder-length dreadlocks cascading across his shoulders, and felt himself getting lost in her for several moments. *The Rage* began to consume him.

She was gasping and wincing. He was hurting her... and he reveling in every second of it. He let go of her throat and her eyes slowly returned to normal. She glared at him, the slightest hint of terror darkening her eyes, but did not stop offering herself to him, stroke-by-stroke. She reached up and grabbed his dreadlocks, pulling him down into a passionate kiss. He returned her kiss with bites on her lips. His *Rage* demanded blood, so he bit deeper. She yelped in the pain of it, causing him to explode deeply within her, shooting towards her soul. He collapsed into her breasts, struggling to find a steady rhythm for his own breath. She wrapped her legs back around him and wiped both the tears from her eyes and the slight trickle of blood from her bottom lip.

"Shit..." he muttered into her skin.

She couldn't find her voice so she stroked his locks instead. After a few deep breaths, he pulled himself away from her and stood up. He looked down and saw her body, twisted up in the sheets, a trickle of blood smearing her face, and smiled, feeling himself stir again.

"And now... your gift," he said with a wry smile.

He turned and walked towards the kitchen, leaving her in bed wondering what more could he have planned. She thought something "special" was the lovely dinner he prepared and this session was an added bonus. *What could he possibly have in mind?* Nicole thought to herself. She inched up in the bed and felt herself getting sleepy. Yawning, she rolled over onto her side and closed her eyes. She heard him walk back into the bedroom, but didn't roll over to face him. She was physically exhausted.

"Do you love me, Luna?"

"Mmmhmmm"

"Do you belong to me?"

"Yes, baby."

"Who owns you?"

"You do."

"Say it. Say my name. Say I own you!"

Detecting an urgency she didn't hear a few moments ago, she rolled over to look at him and see what was going on with him. When she looked up, she saw him standing on the other side of the bed with a long piece of metal that appeared to be burning at the end. It was fashioned in some kind of design and was red, as though it had been sitting on a fire for some time. She instinctively backed up further across the bed.

"W-w-what is that?!" she asked, growing nervous.

"You're mine, yes?"

"Y-y—yes of course, Marcus, but what is this? What are you going to do with that?"
"What did you call me?"

"I'm sorry, Sir. I'm sorry!"

"Come here."

She didn't move any closer to him. She was beginning to put two-and-two together. He was carrying a brand in his hand and he intended to use it on her. That was his surprise. She shook her head, scrambling off of the bed. She did a quick survey of the room and realized he had her blocked in. Any direction she ran, he would catch her.

"Come. Here... NOW!!" he repeated, becoming annoyed with her resistance and hesitation.

"Sir, we haven't discussed this. Are you going to brand me? Sir... I... I don't... I don't want that" she told him, fearful tears forming in her eyes.

"You want what I want. Remember? You committed to that when you surrendered to me."

"But... this isn't what I want."

"You want what I want."

"No, not this time, Sir. I'm sorry but I can't do this."

"You can't or you won't?"

"I won't."

He paused. He rolled his neck, cracking it. He stared at her, feeling himself grow harder as her increasing fear became obvious in the quiver of her voice and the visible trembling of her body.

"You will."

Nicole decided to make a run for it. She knew in her heart she wouldn't get far, but she was going to try. This was it. This was the sign she'd been waiting for. She felt God whispering in her ear, telling her to leave and leave now. She didn't care that she was naked; she was going to get out of there. She dashed around the bed and just then slammed right into his chest. He laughed. He grabbed her with one arm and threw her down on the bed, face down. He used one of his gigantic thighs to hold her down and grabbed the back of her neck with his left hand. She began to flail her arms and squirm feverishly. She couldn't move her legs to kick but she tried.

"This will only hurt for a second, my Luna."

"Marcus, please... don't do this.... Please, baby, don't. I'll do anything else. Please!!" she begged.

Her pleas fell on deaf ears. Marcus was harder than he'd been earlier. He brought the brand down right beneath the right cheek of her buttocks. She screamed out in searing agony, divine music to his ears, and he released himself all over the backs of her thighs, still holding the brand to her skin. Her screams stopped, her silence bringing him back from his frenzied brink. He removed the brand from her skin and took it to the bathroom, throwing it in the tub and turning on the water to cool it off.

He returned to the bedroom to survey his work. She still had not made another sound. He looked closer, examining her. She was still breathing, but appeared to have fainted from the pain. Eh, he thought to himself, isn't the first time. He looked down at the blistering scar, fashioned in the shape of a cursive "M".

He leaned down and kissed the newly-branded cheek.

"Mine" he whispered.

****

"Your 'Bitch', you say?" Marcus questioned with a smirk. "Are you sure about that?"

David took a step forward towards Marcus, "Did I stutter?"

Marcus straightened up. "Oh, you're a tough guy. I see." Marcus sucked his teeth, looked past David at Nicole, then back at David and asked, "Has she tried to run away, yet? She's good for that. She knows nothing about this shit here. Nothing."

As he turned to walk away from David, he muttered "Weak bitch..." under his breath, but not low enough for David and Nicole to miss it.

"Sir, NO!!!!" Nicole yelled out, instinctively knowing what was about to happen. "He's not worth it. Baby please he is not worth it!" and she reached out to grab him as he moved to lunge towards Marcus.

Another couple had been nearby, observing the whole exchange. The man in the couple leaped forward standing in front of David, holding him back as well. As quickly as he lost it, David regained control, checked himself, shrugged off the man and Nicole, and headed towards the exit. Nicole quickly ran after him, fighting back the tears that burned her eyelids. She stole one look back and saw Marcus standing there, clearly angry. She glared at him, turned back forward and kept after David, who was halfway to their car.

David reached the car first and waited for her. He opened her door and she got in and sat silently. He circled around the car and entered on the driver's side. Saying nothing, he put the key into the ignition and turned the car on. When the music began to play, he turned the volume down. He looked over at Nicole, sitting quietly on the passenger's side blinking back tears. He looked away, and took a deep breath.

"I guess that explains the butterfly-covered 'M' branded on your ass"

Lesson Learned

6:17 p.m.

She put the key in the door, but not before she could smell dinner simmering on the stove and dessert baking in the oven. Sighing heavily, Nicole turned the key and opened the door to an even more overwhelmingly delicious aroma. Her eyes closed instinctively as she inhaled deeply. *How much longer can I stand this?*

1 week.

3 days.

19 hours.

She looked at her watch.

17 minutes...

This was the longest period she'd ever been on punishment while serving Him. While she knew she deserved every second of this agony, she still lamented the loss that came with it. She was in the final stretch, however, and she knew she had no choice but to endure it until the end.

****

"No sex, no service, no submission. Two weeks."

"But–"

"Don't you DARE talk back to me, woman. Not...now. Two weeks. Two weeks to think about how keeping things from each other is detrimental to this relationship. Two weeks to think about how embarrassing it is for My Bitch fighting MY fights. Two weeks to think about everything I've shared with you, every way in which I've opened up my entire soul to you, every way in which I've cared for you, honored you, trusted you, and tended to your every wants and need. Two weeks to figure out how to never break my heart in such a way again. Two weeks to remember who you serve and why you're in this with me. Do not dispute me, woman, or I swear before God and everyone we hold dear, you will regret it."

***

Fuck His cooking for being so goddamned good. Shit, she thought to herself.

"Sir?" she called out. No answer.

"Sir?? Where are you?" she asked again. No response.

Sighing again, she removed her coat, hung it in the coat closet, and called out, "David? Where are you?"

"I'm in the bathroom, Nicole. How was your day?"

"It was busy, as usual, but good. What's for dinner?" she asked as she made her way towards the kitchen. "Smells delicious," she commented.

"Pork tenderloins, collard greens with ham, and bacon-wrapped scallops," he answered.

Nicole rolled her eyes up to the heavens and shook her head. She stopped eating pork six weeks prior and David was well-aware. The mindfuck. He'd mastered it. Not only did He disallow her from cooking, He forced her to fend for herself to find sustenance. Nicole's lip involuntarily snarled.

After being temporarily "out of service", she found some of her old habits and ways slipping back into her standard behavior. Not many, but enough to be reminded of why being controlled was essential to her being. He wouldn't let her cook, forced her to watch Him clean and iron His own clothes, and when His back was hurting the other day, He refused to let her massage Him with Tiger Balm. *This hurts me just as much as it hurts you,* He'd said.

Bullshit.

Fuck.

She closed her eyes and leaned forward, her forehead connecting with the door of the refrigerator. She didn't hear David walk towards her, so He startled her when he spoke.

"What? You're not going to eat?" At that moment, Nicole's stomach betrayed her, grumbling loudly.

"Aww, you must be hungry. Here, let me fix you a plate," He offered, taunting her, punishing her.

"No, thank you, David. I'll just grab a snack," she said, opening the refrigerator and looking around for a container of yogurt.

She stole a glance at Him while pretending to look for the yogurt. *Damn, He looks good. Dammit, dammit, dammit,* she chastised herself. She was insanely horny and was not allowed to release, not just with Him, but not even by herself. He'd made that clear too. What made it worse was that this was a stretch of time when neither of them had any traveling to do for work, so they were in their home together, torturous day in and excruciating day out.

"Have you seen my yogurt, Sir?" she asked, casually.

"It's on the door," He responded, without thinking. She smiled. He slipped.

"I don't see it, Sir," she continued, feigning ignorance, pleading with the most subtle hint of seduction.

"Star, it's right..."

He caught himself before He turned around to help her out. He knew He couldn't give into her, even with the slightest connection that might go against her punishment. He focused, instead, on the food in the pots in front of Him.

"Look at me," she softly requested.

He didn't move, not beyond a slight stiffening of His body, which was preparing itself for the inevitable battle brewing.

"I said, 'Look at me', David," she repeated, louder this time. Urgency creeping into her voice.

"No."

"You must..."

"No... Again."

She descended from her bent over position in front of the refrigerator completely onto her knees. She placed her hands on the cool tiles of their kitchen's floor. She began to crawl towards Him, kicking off one shoe after the other. She licked her lips. She'd had enough.

"David..."

David slowly turned around, away from the food, to see His beloved on her knees crawling towards Him, the unmistakable mask of pure lust spread widely across her face.

He swallowed. "Get up, Nicole."

"No." She moved a couple of feet closer to where He stood.

"You must…"

"No…Again."

"Woman, do not do this."

By this point, she was in front of Him. She leaned her head forward, forehead touching the tips of His bare feet. She kissed the top of His left foot, then the top of His right. She gingerly placed her hands around His ankles and massaged them a bit, as she noticed they were swollen. *He's been on His feet all day*, she acknowledged to herself.

"Get. Up."

She shook her head, disregarding His command, and elevated herself, still on her knees, so that her face was directly in front of the battle-losing bulge in His pants. In the next instant, her expert fingers unbuckled, unbuttoned, and withdrew Him from His pleated prison. He grabbed her arms, but it was too late; she drew Him into her mouth as soon as He'd sprung free. She drew the entirety of Him into the deepest reach of her throat, right where He belonged.

He groaned.

She won.

It was difficult to smile while her throat was filled with penis, but she tried. Of course, at that same moment, He looked down upon her and saw a grin trying to show itself and He grabbed a handful of her hair in response, yanking her head back, freeing Himself. His resolve hastily returned.

"You want this dick, huh? You conniving, petulant brat, you want this dick so bad, huh? Don't you? DON'T YOU??!"

Before she could answer, she felt His palm across the left side of her face three seconds before He shoved Himself back into her mouth and down her throat. His left hand still gripped her hair and His right hand now gripped the left side of her neck. Slowly at first, He thrust Himself in and out of her mouth, allowing Himself to savor the pleasure of it. Hearing her moan a few times, He knew she was enjoying it entirely too much, so He quickened the pace. He craved her tears.

She lifted her hands to wrap around Him, but He stopped her immediately.

"Put your fucking hands down and take it!! You better… fucking… take it… since you wanted it so fucking bad. So bad that you disregarded my punishment. So bad that you disrespect my commands. So bad that you can't even spend two weeks doing as I demanded of you. Put your hands behind your back!!"

She laced her fingers behind her back as her eyes shut tight. She knew she'd brought this assault on herself.

"Open your eyes. Look at me. You look at me...now."

She looked up and met His gaze. The tears formed as she saw His eyes shift from raging red anger to the sadness of unbearable hurt.

"Why didn't you just tell me?" He pled. "Why didn't you just tell me who he was and what happened, baby?" She felt Him ease up on His assault of her throat. More tears fell from her eyes.

"We promised to share everything. Everything!! I opened myself up to you completely. More than I ever have with any woman before. Was he that important to you? Huh? That motherfucker wasn't SHIT!! He was NOTHING!!!" He tried to get deeper into her throat. He wanted to fuck her soul into penance.

"Did you love him more than me?? Do you still love him??"

He held Himself for a few seconds, deep in her throat. He could feel and hear her gagging. He grew harder. Her suffering excited Him, even amid His most vulnerable plea. She tried to shake her head to indicate negative responses to His questions, but He held her head so tight, she could not budge. She reached up and grabbed His wrists. He knew this meant she was struggling, but in that moment, He wanted her to feel His pain. He eased up a bit more, but He didn't let go.

As she felt Him softening, she relaxed her jaw even more. He needed this, she knew. She also knew that there would be a lot of work to be done for each of them to forgive her for keeping Marcus a secret from Him. She'd told Him bits and pieces about her past, but she'd never gone into depth about Marcus. Part of her secrecy was because she didn't want to rehash the memories, as they were intense and painful. Part of it was that she didn't want Him feeling insecure, as men sometimes feel when they're new to The Life and their women have more experience. She didn't want Him comparing Himself to a man who deserved no such consideration.

"I love you... SO fucking much... I can't be without you, baby. God, woman, don't you know that?"

He let go of her neck and her hair and halted His thrusts. He slid down into a heap in front of her. She reached up, both to embrace Him, and to turn off the burners on the stove, as she'd begun to smell a burning odor. She pulled Him into her arms, whispering "I'm sorry..." at least ten to fifteen times. "I'm sorry, I'm sorry, I'm sorry my love," she cried into His arms.

He buried His face into her neck and wrapped His arms around her waist. He squeezed her for a moment before He began to grab at her clothes. His fever pitched as His lust boiled to the surface. He tried unbuttoning her blouse, one of His favorites, but gave up when He couldn't get His fingers to work in preservation of the garment. He ripped it open and pulled her bra up, freeing her breasts. He palmed them and pressed against her, pushing her back onto the cold floor.

He leaned forward, mouth descending on her left nipple, sucking it in gently as His tongue swirled around her nipple. Her soft moans let Him know that she was ready for more. He switched nipples, sucking and biting the right nipple while His finger tweaked her left. He positioned Himself between on top of her, then pushing her legs wide apart, He nestled in between her. Because she was on punishment, her panties were a rare barrier but not for long.

He yanked them down, dragging them off of her legs. She kicked them across the kitchen floor. He repositioned Himself between her legs and entered her swiftly. One week, three days, nineteen hours, thirty-nine minutes He'd denied Himself the pleasure of being home inside of His beloved, brightest Star. As He moved inside of her, He watched as her eyes rolled up into her head as she received Him, her lover, her friend, her owner, her One.

The pace quickened as He felt Himself coming close to the end. David knew He wouldn't last long and He didn't care. He needed to fill her up and remind her, and maybe Himself, that she belonged to Him now. Now, and for as long as HE decided. Looking down at her tear-stained face, half-closed eyes, puckered lips, and pulsating neck, He decided then, that it would be forever.

He came inside of her with a force He'd never experienced before that moment. She wrapped her legs tightly around His waist, drawing Him in closer than was possible. He collapsed on top of her, face again buried in her neck. Their breaths were short and rapid, balancing each other with alternating inhales and exhales. Their bodies began to relax as the heat began to escape them. David leaned up and looked down at Nicole's face again. She met His eyes and smiled.

"Marry me?"

Her eyes widened briefly. Then, she slowly raised an eyebrow, saying nothing. He smiled down at her, shaking His head.

"You WILL marry me, Star."

She smiled, slyly, biting her bottom lip. She stared intently into His eyes.

"As you wish, Sir."

9:43 a.m.

"Ayyeeeeeeee shiiiiit!!!!"

He screamed in a high-pitched voice she'd only heard once or twice before. He grabbed both sides of her head by her ears and squeezed as He released His morning load down her throat where it belonged. He pulled himself out and covered her mouth, so she wouldn't spill a drop.

"Dammit, girl, wooo shit!! Unnnhhh.... I... you...how...damn!"

He stuttered, unable to form a complete thought. He moaned, body still quivering, toes curling almost until cramping. She gently removed His hand, licking her lips, and raised her head to meet His eyes but found them closed. He was panting and she could see beads of sweat across His forehead. The heat in their apartment was overwhelming at times and this morning was no different. She waited a bit before saying anything.

"You may speak," He mumbled.

"Merry Christmas, Sir," she greeted Him. "How do You feel?" she asked, receiving only a muffled grunt in response.

She smiled, excited because this was their first Christmas together as an engaged couple. They'd not yet announced the news to anyone in their families and planned to tell His family this evening at dinner. Normally, she didn't make a big deal out of the holiday season because she was often working or too tired to make any big efforts. She listened to holiday music and bought gifts for her friends' children, of course, but didn't quite fall into the entirety of the "Christmas Spirit".

This year was different because not only had He collared her, He made a promise to marry her...eventually. Neither of them was in any particular rush to begin the wedding-planning process and each liked the idea of a longer engagement, as they were still ascending in their careers and had major projects on their respective tables. Still, Nicole enjoyed glancing at her ring finger as much as fingering her collars, feeling completeness in her connection to her One.

David rolled over, muttering "Breakfast..." before burying His face into a pillow. Nicole quickly scrambled out of the bed and headed to the kitchen. While He dozed, she prepared His favorite breakfast of Belgian waffles, fried chicken wings, and cheese grits. When they were still dating, she'd made this meal and He deemed it "perfect". Now, she only made it on special occasions and holidays to preserve the "special" element of it. Her mental Rolodex of His favorite things remained well-organized, as her job was to remember everything that made Him happiest and provided Him with the greatest satisfaction.

She placed His breakfast on the dining room table and went back to the bedroom to wake Him up to eat. She paused at the door and took a moment to look Him over. He'd just gotten back from a 10-day business trip, hitting three cities in that time. She picked Him up from the airport at 12:30 a.m. and they were both too tired to do anything but collapse into bed and fall deeply asleep. She knew how to wake Him up though.

"Come here," He called to her, face still half-buried in the pillow. Nicole made her way to the side of the bed.

"Kneel."

She immediately descended to her knees and lowered her head, placing her hands behind her back. David sat Himself up and dangled His legs over the side of the bed. He sat for a moment, staring down at the top of her head. She was poised so perfectly still and positioned the way He required...

Beautiful.

His.

He got out of bed and walked around her to one of the closets in the hallway. He returned with an immaculately-wrapped thin jewelry box in His hand and stood before her.

"You are my greatest gift, Star. You are my prize... you are my strength... you are my faith... you are Mine," He said, slowly and deliberately. He lifted her face up with one hand.

"Look at me."

She looked up and met His gaze.

"Merry Christmas," He said, handing her the box. He leaned against the edge of the bed as she grabbed the gift gleefully.

"Ooooh, what is it, Sir?" she asked, shaking it by her ear to see if she could detect it first that way.

"Just open it, woman," He said, laughing at her as she ripped open the paper.

Pale blue box. Tiffany & Co. Of course. She'd been eyeing the Tiffany Infinity Bracelet for some time, so she figured He picked it up for her. She opened the box and gasped, as she saw not the bracelet, but what appeared to be a custom-made Infinity necklace, which she knew was not simply a necklace. She ran her fingers along the double chains of the collar and lifted the Infinity charm. She felt ridges behind it and turned it over to find an inscription, *"Mine."* The simple inscription she'd come to expect on each of His gifts was neatly engraved in delicate cursive.

"Sir..." she whispered, "This is... This is beautiful. My goodness...Oh, but it is too much!" As soon as she said the words, she regretted them.

SMACK A swift hand came down upon her left buttock with lightning speed. She yelped and jumped a bit.

"You know better."

"I'm sorry."

"Mmmmhmmmm."

"It's beautiful. Thank you so much, Sir."

"Allow me..."

He took the box from her and removed the collar. He stood behind her and gingerly fastened it around her neck. Leaning down, He kissed her on the cheek, wrapped His right hand around her throat, clutching it tight and whispered, "Mine." She closed her eyes, breathed in deeply, reveling in the intimacy of the moment. She exhaled and affirmed, "Always."

"Get up. I'm hungry. Feed me, woman," He commanded with a smile and a soft pat on her behind. He helped her up and they went to enjoy their Christmas breakfast together.

*****

4:35 p.m.

"Your mama hates me."

"She doesn't hate you."

"Yes, she does."

"I promise you, she doesn't hate you. She just doesn't... get it." They sat in the car, parked outside of the house He lived in as a teenager. Nicole hadn't removed her seat belt yet, and was visibly nervous and tense.

"She thinks I'm weak."

"I know you're not."

"I want her to know that."

"She does, in her own way. She just has trouble accepting what it is that we do because of everything she went through with my father, yanno?"

"I know..."

Nicole sighed and braced herself to deal with David's mother, Janice. She'd only met her twice before and each time, she bristled at the jabs and rather mean quips Janice made in response to the ways in which Nicole and David interacted. She learned, earlier on, that David's father caused all kinds of trouble for his mother for several years before she eventually took David, His older brother Jonathan, and left him for good. He had a serious gambling problem, and it cost them more than David ever knew.

They struggled a lot in the immediate years after, but David would come to understand that His mother did the best she could for all of them. It was several years before David was able to face His father and several years after that before He could bring Himself to forgive him. These days, He maintained a solid relationship with his father and supported him as he did his best to turn his life around.

Because of her experiences with David's father, Janice had become a hardened woman in her older age. She was a no-nonsense, blunt woman who was never afraid to speak her mind and give her opinion about any and everything. She could be rather dismissive, especially of women she deemed "weak". Since leaving David's father, Janice had not been in a steady, long-term relationship. She'd had a few lovers here and there, or at least David believed so, but she never introduced any one man as "Her Man". She even said, *"Ain't no man ever gonna own me again!"*

David wanted His mother to be happy with someone, but knew she carried a lot of anger, hurt, and bitterness still. David could count on His hands the number of times in His adult years He remembered seeing her smile. Unfortunately, the nature of His relationship with Nicole, which He never hid, didn't exactly earn His mother's approval. His brother, Jonathan, didn't understand it, but shrugged it off because it wasn't any of his business.

David had no intentions of changing His behavior with Nicole, however, because He was living freely in His truth; she was going to have to respect His choices.

"Star, it's going to be fine. She'll be happy to hear our good news, I promise," He cajoled. He lifted her left hand and kissed her ring finger. "She has her issues but she just wants her boys to be happy. You make me happy... and it's Christmas. She loves Christmas."

Nicole took a deep breath and nodded. She was to trust in Him and His guidance, always. She smiled at Him. "Let's go!"

"Yeah, let's go. We're late, your fault," He said, with a sly smirk. She blushed, knowing they were late because she got... hungry... again.

The front door was open and there were several people in the living room, including Jonathan, his wife, Darlene, their two sons, Junior and D.J. Nicole could hear Janice's laughter from the kitchen, so she took off her coat and glanced at David.

He gave her a nod and she proceeded to the kitchen to offer her help, greeting family as she walked through the living room. David hung up their coats and settled in with His young nephews as He and Jonathan caught up on what was going on with their respective jobs.

Nicole entered the kitchen and saw Janice and two women she didn't recognize. She smiled and waved, making her presence known.

"See, now, this here is my youngest baby's girlfriend, Nicole," Janice said to her friends, Carol and Brenda, as she waved Nicole over for a hug. Nicole walked over to her, hesitant in her embrace, but she welcomed it nonetheless. She hugged the other ladies, too, greeting them with a warm, albeit skeptical smile.

"It's nice to meet you. Can I help with anything?" she asked, looking around the kitchen to see what she could get her hands into. She began rolling up her sleeves when Janice surprisingly grabbed her left arm.

"Ohhhh myyyy gooodnessssss!!!!!" she yelled loud enough for the entire house to hear. "What is this on your...? Did my boy...? DAVID!!! David you get in here right now!!!" she yelled towards the living room.

Nicole was caught off-guard, but didn't feel any negativity. Janice was smiling and staring at the ring on her finger, waving Nicole's hand around for Carol and Brenda to see. "Y'all see this rock?? Whewwww my boy did good with this one!!"

Just then David entered the kitchen, confused, looking around to see what was on fire. "Mama, what's wrong? What happened??"

"Nothing is wrong! Come here and give your mama a hug!!"

She dropped Nicole's hand and made her way over to her youngest son, pulling Him into a strong embrace. Like Nicole, David was startled by the gesture, as He always knew His mother to be more reserved and less affectionate.

"Mama, you ok?" He asked, just as skeptical as Nicole.

"I'm fine, baby! Don't you have something to tell me? Hmmm?"

She was smiling wide, and while David wondered where it was coming from, He rolled with it, not wanting to dampen His mother's good mood.

"Ahhh well yes. A few weeks ago, I asked Nicole to be my wife and she agreed. Well, more like I told her she was going to marry me and she accepted it," He said with a wink towards Nicole. She chuckled and shook her head, walking towards His extended arm. She nestled in by His side and nodded her head.

"Yes, David told me I was going to marry Him. How could I say No?" She instinctively fingered her new collar and smiled.

"Well congratulations to you both!" Carol said. "Janice, you know you're gonna have a good ole time planning this wedding! You know, Pastor Wright would have no–"

"Whoa, whoa, whoa, ladies. Slow down," David interrupted. "Nicole and I are not getting married anytime soon and we haven't discussed any plans remotely related to a wedding. We don't even know if we're having a big wedding or if we're gonna go to Vegas and elope," He said. Janice glared at Him, shifted her eyes to Nicole, then back to Him.

"Well now, what you mean y'all ain't getting married anytime soon? How long you plan on being engaged? You know you younger folks don't know anything about tradition. You wanna do things all new and different. Elope? That's not a real marriage. You need to get married in church, by a good preacher and under the eyes of God, ya hear me?"

"Mama, I don't think we need to get into this right now," David responded.

"I don't see why not, being as though you brought the girl in here with this fancy ass ring and didn't even tell me until weeks later," she chastised.

"Well, we wanted to surprise you," Nicole chimed in. She felt a pinch on her lower back from David, meaning she needed to stay out of this one. She lowered her head.

"Mama, we're going to do this the way we want to and that is final," David stated, firmer in His tone.

"You sound just like your father," Janice said, dismissing Him with a wave of her hand. She turned back to the collard greens that were finished cooking on the stove and began dishing them into a serving bowl. "You know, he was just as stubborn as can be too."

"I'm well-aware of how Dad can be, Mama," David replied with a sigh. "Just be happy for us, please?"

"I am happy for you, baby," Janice said. "Nicole is a lovely woman and it's about time you settle down and start a family of your own," she said with her back to Him.

"Mamaaaa," He groaned.

Nicole smiled to herself, seeing a new side of her Sir that she wasn't used to. Clearly, He was a mama's boy, and Janice was a weak spot for Him. She didn't mind it, though, because He'd never made her feel like she was in competition with Janice. She was getting to see how His mother, or His connection to her after all they'd been through, made Him vulnerable. She appreciated it.

David whispered in Nicole's ear, "Upstairs, second door to your left. Now." She excused herself a few seconds later, left David talking with His mother a bit more and made her way upstairs. The second door on the left was a nice-sized bathroom, larger than the one in their apartment. It was decorated mostly in lilac and yellow and had a large, old-fashioned, deep marble tub with claws. Nicole fantasized about how wonderful bubble baths must be in such a tub. She opened the medicine cabinet and glanced around, not to be nosy, just to occupy herself. She jumped when the door opened and David came in.

"Kneel."

"What?"

"Did I stutter?"

"David, we're in your–"

"What did you call me?"

"Sir, I'm sorry," she apologized looking around. "Sir, this is your mama's house!"

"Quiet. Kneel."

She hesitated a few seconds too long, she realized, when she felt His hand around her throat, clutching.

"I said... Kneel."

She dropped to her knees with His hand still around her throat.

"Now... did I tell you to speak back there in the kitchen?"

She said nothing, and lowered her head instead.

"Answer me."

"No."

"No, what?"

"No, Sir."

"I didn't think so." He moved behind her and grabbed a fistful of her hair, yanking her head back.

"So my bad girl thinks that because she is around my family, she can get out of line? Is that it?"

"No, Sir."

"Well you certainly had a lot to say down there."

"I'm sorry, Sir. I won't speak out of turn around your mother again."

"Oh I know you won't," He agreed.

With His free hand, He plucked her lips three times, which was His standard discipline for when she spoke out of turn. She winced a bit, then licked her lips. Her pussy was wet. He knew it.

"Get up."

She stood up quickly. As soon as she was to her feet, He bent her over so she could grab the edge of the tub to stabilize herself. In less than thirty seconds, her skirt was around her waist and He was buried deep in her, His stroke frenzied.

"I swear… that woman… drives me so… fucking crazy…sometimes," He growled while plowing into her. "I swear if she wasn't my Mama, I'd tell her to shut the fuck up!"

Nicole said nothing. She realized this was less about her speaking out and more about Him needing to release His frustration. She, of course, was His to use as He needed. She spread her legs a bit wider to stabilize herself. He was definitely going in fast, hard, and deep. After a couple of minutes, she lifted her right leg and put it on the edge of the tub, giving Him deeper access.

"She just…needs… to let me…do… what the fuck… I want to do… with My Bitch….FUCK!!" He grabbed her waist and pulled her back onto Him, never breaking the rhythm or connection. Nicole moaned and He slapped His hand over her mouth.

"Shut. The. Fuck. Up," He growled into her ear.

She was so wet and ready, she came quickly all over Him. A few minutes later, He exploded deep inside of her. Just as He was finishing dumping His load, they heard young D.J.'s voice yelling out, "Uncle Davidddddddd? Where are youuu??? I gotta pee!!!" He followed with a strong pounding on the door, which elicited a giggle from Nicole.

"You nephew has to pee, Sir," she said, chuckling as she lowered and smoothed out her skirt.

"Ha ha," He responded. "Just a minute, D.J.!" He called to the young boy.

"Okkkkk!" D.J. responded, sounding like he was going back downstairs. Nicole turned around and bent down to lick Him clean, but He'd already zipped up His pants.

"Fix your face, nasty girl" He said, knowing she was pouting without even looking. "Can't have you talking to my Mama with nut on your breath," He finished, shaking His head at her. She stood in front of the mirror and fussed with her hair, which was tussled after He grabbed it.

"You are so fucking nasty. You horny fucker!" David said.

"You like it."

"Indeed."

They laughed together. Nicole slipped out of the bathroom first and David waited a moment before following her. When He got downstairs, He heard new voices and went into the living room. He saw His mother in a tight embrace with an older, well-dressed man. He looked for Nicole and saw her standing, oddly still, by the entrance to the kitchen.

"Baby, come here and meet my friend, Joseph!" Janice called out, waving David over to greet her new beau. "I invited him over for dinner and he brought his son with him," she said with a wide smile pointing towards the door. David looked over and immediately understood why Nicole stood almost frozen in the corner.

"David, meet–" Janice began.

"Marcus..." Nicole finished.

December 22, 2002 4:35 a.m.

"Annie Christian wanted...to be number one... but her kingdom never comes... thy will be done."

David sat quietly at the deserted intersection, waiting for the light to change from red to green. He was exhausted, having not fallen asleep until after midnight and receiving an alarming phone call at 2 a.m. He'd spent most of the week working on a final project that was due today, getting little sleep, and eating even less. Graduate school was kicking his ass but it was a necessary step on his path to success. At least he'd mapped it out that way. He was 25, one semester away from obtaining his MBA, and here he was on his way to pick his father, Eric, up from some unknown seedy motel almost 2 hours away from where he stayed near campus.

He could barely keep his eyes open, so he cranked up vintage Prince on his stereo and sipped his coffee. *I'm so sick of this shit,* he thought to himself. It wasn't the first time he'd been summoned out of bed to help his father and he was sure it wouldn't be the last. Having just gotten in on the increasingly popular cellular phone trend, he found himself adjusting to being so readily accessible to everyone, especially his father. As he tapped his fingers on the steering wheel, he wished he hadn't given his father the number to his Nokia cell phone.

"Annie Christian was a whore...always looking for some fun..."

David made a right when the light changed and pulled into the motel's parking lot. All of the slots were occupied, cars varying from high end to run down, and the curtains were drawn in most of the windows. He pulled his car alongside a navy blue Lexus with police plates. He shook his head when he saw Eric leaned up against a large dumpster. Next to him was a too-thin woman in a tattered silver sequined dress holding a large bottle of some sort. She was half-standing, half-leaning on his father, whose eyes appeared to be closed. David turned off the engine, shut off the lights, and took a deep breath.

"Dad. Time to go home!" he called, as he stepped out of the vehicle. He took long strides towards his father, annoyance turning more into disgust with every step.

"Dad..." he repeated. "Let's go," David said as he reached to help Eric stand up straighter.

"Aye, baby boy," slurred the woman in a half-hearted attempt to be flirtatious, "You shole do get your looks from yo daddy, don't ya?" Turning to David's father, she continued, "Why you ain't tell me you had a son this damned fine, daddy? Sheeeet, I might have to trade you in for a younger model!"

She cackled loudly and David could smell the Wild Irish Rose on her breath from the bottle she held in her hand. He instinctively covered his nose with his hand.

"Whuuu...whut you tryna say? My bref stank?" She coughed into her hand and sniffed, backing up at the shock of what she smelled. "Oh shit, well... you ain't nevuh lied, ha haaaaa," she agreed with another cackle that turned into a harsh cough.

"Bitch, if you don't shut the fuck up and leave my boy alone!" commanded Eric, eyes slowly opening, words slurring slightly indicating he'd had more than a few sips of the same drink.

"What you gonna do, muthafucka???" she asked, backing away from him and holding her arms up.

"Bitch, I will beat yo ass into next week!!" he retorted, as he reached for her throat with both hands.

David lunged forward and grabbed his father's arms before his hands could wrap around her throat. Having witnessed his father do this more than once with his mother, David knew it would get ugly really quickly. The woman yelped and turned around to run away. As David heard the click-clack of her cheap shoes against the pavement, he wrapped one arm around Eric's back, put one of Eric's arms over his shoulders, and practically dragged his father back to his car. He got him situated and belted in and made his way back to the driver's seat.

When he'd turned the engine back on, he lowered the music, took another deep breath and looked at Eric, who was slumped against the back of the passenger's seat.

"Take me to your mother's house," he said in a voice barely above a whisper.

"Not this time, dad."

"Boy, I said take me to you goddamned mother's house. What the fuck is your problem?"

"Dad, it's almost dawn. She's asleep."

"She'll be awake when we get there."

"Dad, I'm not doing this to her again."

"She'll let me in. She always does..."

David sighed, knowing what his father said was true. Despite having left him and moved herself and her sons away from Eric, David learned that she still occasionally let him come to her home and spend a night or three there. She bathed him, gave him clean clothes, and fed him, probably cursing him out the entire time. But still, she let him in. Every time.

"Dad, why can't you just leave mom alone and let her move on with her life? Why are you still trapping her with your shit?"

"Don't you cuss me boy!"

"You wanna talk about me cursing when you're sitting in *my* car, pissy drunk, unable to stand straight, and in need of a ride? Oh, oh that's just great!"

"You better get to driving. Will take at least an hour to get to Janice's house," he continued, ignoring David completely. "Make sure you use that sella phone thing and call her to let her know we're coming. She'll have a plate ready for me. Damn, I'm hungry. Whew!"

David pulled out of the motel parking lot and began driving. He was unsure of where he was going, but he knew he was not going to take Eric anywhere near his mother. Maybe she wasn't fully able to turn him away, and David tried to understand that connection, but he wasn't going to enable it. He thought about taking him to his own apartment, but the rest he needed influenced the decision against that. He thought of the hotel strip a few miles from campus and figured he could get him a room for the night to sleep it off.

"Yanno, I ain't shit."

"Come on, Dad..."

"No, no, no, lemme finish. I ain't shit. I. Ain't. Shit!! Now ya mama, that's a helluva lady there. Wheweee what a woman!" Eric paused before continuing, turning to look out of the window. He continued, quieter, "I really fucked that up, didn't I?" He looked back at David, as if waiting for a real answer. David said nothing.

"See, your mama is one of those strong women. She didn't take no shit. She was a no-nonsense, go-getter type, yanno what I mean? She was about her business when I met her. Had her shit together! Was finishing school, had a job lined up, was really gonna make something of herself. I had to have her. Had to... You just don't let a woman like that pass you by. Ooooh and she was fine as she wanted to be!" Eric paused to chuckle to himself and appeared to be stuck in a memory for a few seconds.

"That woman saved my life."

"What do you mean, Dad?"

"Just what I said. Ya mama saved my life. I wasn't shit then. Hell, I still ain't shit, but... for the time God blessed me with being with her, she saved me. Even when I treated her like shit, she loved me. Took me back. Fed me. Took care of me. I ain't deserve *none* of that shit, ya hear me? I cheated on her. Beat on her. Gambled away all her money. My money. Everything..."

Eric slumped further down into his seat, feeling the weight of his confessions. He reached out and placed his hand over his son's on the steering wheel. When he could have squeezed it, he pulled back, defeated. Intoxicated. Sick. Wasted. Life, wasted.

"I remember," David said, finally.

"I... I know you do son. You and your brother. He still won't talk to me, yanno? I tried calling him a few times but...he won't call me back. Why won't he call me back, son?" Eric looked caught at the intersection of sadness, dejection, and hope.

"He'll come around, Dad."

"No, he won't. I don't even blame him. Listen...you got a girlfriend yet?"

"No."

"Well, good. Keep your head in those books. Women take a lot of out of you. They can change you, for the better if you let them. For worse if you let yourself go too far."

"Dad, I'm not trying to have a relationship convo with you right now. I'm really not. You are the *last* person who needs to be doling out relationship advice."

"Maybe you can learn from my fuck ups, son. Maybe I can be of some use to you somehow..."

David looked straight ahead and focused on driving. Eric said little for the next 20 minutes or so, and David turned up the volume on the car stereo.

"Whenever I feel like giving up. Whenever my sunshine turns to grey. Whenever my hopes and dreams are aimed in wrong directions, she's always there, telling me how much she cares..."

"When you find that one...that one woman that makes you wish for more hours in each day, makes the sun shine brighter on rainy days... that woman who, who really just lifts every single part of you up towards the heavens...because...because she believes you to be as close to God as she'll get... That woman who wipes your tears, irons your clothes, and feeds you your favorite meals, laughs at your stupid, stupid jokes, and opens the door for you... even when you've done next to nothing to make her feel special... don't let her go. Don't fuck that up. Don't abuse her. Don't use her. Don't you dare take that woman for granted or mistreat her because believe me, oh boy believe me, son, she is the ONE! Ya gotta take care of a woman like that, buy her nice things, take her out to nice places, come home at a decent hour, and rub her feet every now and then. I swear to you, boy, that woman will worship the ground you walk on if you just take care of her. Just...take... care of her, you hear me?"

"Yes, Dad. I hear you."

I hear you.

****

Christmas Day 2012

"Nicole?! Baby girrrrrl!! Long time no see, long long time!" Joseph exclaimed as he walked over to Nicole, who stood practically frozen in a corner of the living room.

With extended arms, he pulled her into an embrace that startled her out of her stunned silence. She obliged him and returned the hug with what little energy she could muster. Looking over his shoulder, she could see Marcus looking almost as uncomfortable as she felt and for some reason, she relaxed a bit. He was avoiding eye contact with both her and David.

"Girl, let me look at you! Whewwwweeee! You're looking good girl! Lost a lot of that chubby chub you had going on there, didn't ya? Not that you looked bad," he corrected himself.

"But wow! You look like one of them Next Top Models of America or whatever they call them girls on that big headed one's show. Doesn't she have a big head? What's her name? Tyesha? Tyricka?"

"Tyra, Tyra Banks" Nicole responded, chuckling. She couldn't help but laugh. Joseph had always been the humorous charmer. She didn't realize until then that she'd actually missed him a bit. She glanced over at David who stared at Marcus, watching his every move. She could see His jaw twitching and she grew concerned about His next moves.

"David? Let me introduce you to Joseph, M..M.. Marcus's father," she began, waving David over. "Joseph, this is my fiancé, David, who I'm sure you've heard a bit about from Janice," she continued with a smile. She was determined to de-escalate this situation before it became volatile.

"Well now, yes, I have heard about Janice's sons," Joseph said extending his hand to shake David's. "She didn't mention David having a fiancée as beautiful as you," he continued with a smile.

"That's because we just announced it today!" Nicole decided to not contain her excitement and she may have cranked it up a notch, given the new company. She extended her hand out to show off the engagement ring Janice had gawked over not long ago.

"Well damn, you can see that rock from over here," Marcus chimed in.

He was staring at the three of them from across the room, saying nothing until now. Marcus's words brought Joseph out of his moment of reverie and he stepped back from Nicole, as if remembering his allegiance. He let go of her hand, which he'd been holding while examining her ring.

"That's a nice ring you have there, young lady. Too bad you're not marrying my boy here," he said with half of a laugh.

"Pop..." Marcus began.

He glanced at David and made a shrugging gesture. David felt His own shoulders relaxing a bit. Janice, looking back and forth between her new beau, his son, Marcus, who she was meeting for the first time, her own son, and her son's new fiancée, finally spoke up.

"What in the hell is going on here? Can someone please tell me how y'all know each other?" she asked, confused and feeling left out.

"Mama, it seems as though the world is far smaller than we could ever imagine. Nicole and Marcus used to be an item, many *many* years ago," David explained to his mother, a wry smile creeping to His lips. "It's fine, Mama, don't worry. I only recently met Marcus myself. Chance meeting at a social club. Didn't think that I'd see him again after Nicole and I went home that night, though."

"Oh?... OH! Oh well...well goodness," she stumbled, trying to find the right words to say. "Well everyone get washed up, and let's eat before this food gets cold. I didn't slave over that hot stove since yesterday for nothing!" Janice made her way towards the kitchen and Nicole followed her to help bring the food out.

Marcus, David, and Joseph all stood still for a moment, glancing back and forth at each other, not sure what to say next.

"Awww shit...", Darlene mumbled.

"Mommy, you said a bad word!" her son Junior chastised.

"I'm sorry, baby, Mommy didn't mean to curse...but this is about to be some shit," she apologized with a laugh. Jonathan shook his head as he stood up. "I'll show you gentlemen where the bathroom is," he said as began walking towards the stairs.

"Oh I know where it is," Joseph insisted. David shot him a quick look. Clearly, this wasn't Joseph's first time in this home and David realized His mother has been keeping a secret from Him for some time.

"I'll use the downstairs bathroom. Son, you go upstairs. It's the second door on the left," Joseph instructed.

Marcus made his way upstairs and Jonathan and Darlene got their family situated at the table. David stood by His seat, awaiting Nicole's return. She returned a minute or so later, carrying a casserole dish filled with Janice's "famous" macaroni and cheese. She caught David's eye, smiled at Him, and went back into the kitchen to get another dish. David felt Himself relax even more.

When Marcus returned, he took a seat across from where David stood, affording him the opportunity to address David, face-to-face. He sat down, and when Nicole and Janice brought more dishes to the table, he didn't bother to stand up.

David remained standing.

After all of the dishes were on the table, David pulled out Nicole's chair and she sat down. He took His own seat next to her and sat back and she began to prepare His plate.

"Mama, I must say you outdid yourself this year. Everything looks delicious!"

David felt His stomach rumbling, an indication that He truly missed His mother's home cooking. Nicole could really cook things up in the kitchen, but there was something about His mother's meals that made Him feel warm inside.

"Yes, ma'am, I must say everything will find its way to my plate today," Marcus chimed in, patting his stomach.

"You should get started fixing your own plate, then, Marcus," Nicole said as she dished a heaping helping of macaroni and cheese onto David's plate. "Would you like more, Sir?" she asked Him, sweetly.

"No, baby, that's enough. Thank you," David responded as His hand gently made its way up her back. "You take such great care of me, Star." David looked straight ahead at Marcus and smirked. "Here you go," he said, passing Marcus a serving spoon. "Dig in!"

Marcus took the serving spoon and began fixing his plate, no trace of a smile anywhere on his face. Nicole tried to hide her own smile, but David didn't.

"So, Marcus, I haven't heard much about you...like, *at all*. Why don't you tell me about yourself?" David began. "What do you do for a living?"

"Well, I'm in construction and contracting. Lu–," he paused. "Nicole helped me start my own contracting business when we were together. Gave me the seed money," he explained, looking at her. "I owe her my life, really."

"You paid me back, with interest, Marcus. You owe me nothing," she responded.

David looked at her with a side glance, her mouthiness prickling and tickling him simultaneously. Nicole placed David's plate in front of Him and proceeded to make her own. "Make sure you try Janice's collard greens. She doesn't use pork and they are to *die* for."

"I'll keep that in mind," he responded. "So, yeah, I'm in construction. Not balling like you, though, brothaman. That ring had to set you back quite a bit."

"Not at all actually," David responded. "In fact, my *brother*, Jonathan, knows some people and well, price isn't an issue when it comes to someone priceless," David continued. He leaned over and whispered to Nicole. *Eat.* She began to eat her food and it was then that Marcus noticed the glimmer around her neck.

"Finger blinging, neck blinging, seems this guy here has got you on lock, baby girl," he said, trying to make light of the sting he couldn't help but feel.

"Oh like you wouldn't believe," David said immediately.

His hand went to the back of Nicole's neck and His fingers traced her collar. He looked back at Marcus and mouthed one word: *Mine.* David cocked His head to the side a bit as Marcus glared at Him for a moment, and then lowered his own head to focus on his meal.

David heard a sound He'd not heard in many years, His mother's giggle. He looked down the table to see her giggling after what seemed like a stolen kiss from Joseph. It was Christmas Day and He couldn't remember that last time He'd seen Janice look so genuinely happy. She was glowing, laughing, and her smile was lighting up the room. If it were possible, He'd say her food even tasted better than in previous years. *I can't fuck this up*, He thought to Himself. He ran His hand through Nicole's hair and kissed her temple. She stopped before taking a bite of food and turned into the kiss, smiling. Theirs was contagious because Jonathan pulled his wife, Darlene, in for a kiss right after that.

Marcus focused on his collard greens.

"So when's the wedding, kids?" Joseph asked for the opposite end of the table.

"We're not sure yet," David responded.

"What's the hold up, man?" Marcus inquired, between bites. He looked at Nicole. "She scared or something?" He winked at her. David felt her stiffen. Nicole grabbed His thigh under the table and squeezed. His jaw was clenched again.

"Scared? What does she have to be scared of? My brand... of love isn't anything to fear. Not at all," David replied.

"Well you know how some of these women can be. They can't handle the pressure...run at the first sign of trouble straight into the arms of the next man," Marcus countered.

"Awww shit," Darlene said under her breath. Jonathan shot her a dirty look. She pretended to focus on her plate, pushing her fork around, shaking her head.

"I'll be right back," David said, standing up to excuse Himself. As He stood, Nicole followed suit, as was the expected behavior. David said, "Sit," and He headed to the stairs to go up to the bathroom. Nicole sat back down and tried to focus on eating, but found her appetite completely gone.

"What's the matter, baby girl? Why are you acting so cold? Feeling a chill down below?" He pointed to the pocket on his shirt, where Nicole saw a red satiny cloth sticking out. "You missing something? Found these in the bathroom on the floor, by the tub," he said in a hushed tone. He quickly pulled the red panties out, balled them in his hand, brought them to his nose, and inhaled.

Nicole grabbed the glass of wine before her, brought it to her lips, and whispered back with a slight smirk, "Come now, Marcus, you know me better than that." She took a long sip from her wine glass. "I wasn't wearing any to begin with," she continued, looking him directly in his eyes.

Just then, Janice let out another infectious giggle and Marcus's eyes shot to her, the horror spreading across his face. As he seemed to pale a bit, Nicole choked on her wine, from the knot of laughter bubbling in her throat. Wine shot from her nose all over her plate and her face turned beet red. She alternated between laughing and coughing so loudly, she caught Janice's and Joseph's attention. Both shot up from their seats and rushed down to see if she was alright. Marcus quickly shoved the panties into his pants pocket. Just then David returned to the table to see the commotion.

"Baby, you OK?" He said, rushing to her aid, patting her on the back.

"Don't pat her back, boy, you'll only make it worse," Janice cautioned. Nicole waved both of them off and began to wipe the tears from her eyes.

"It's nothing, nothing really. I'm fine. Wine just went down the wrong pipe," she said when she caught a steady breath. Janice and Joseph made their ways back to their end of the table. Nicole dabbed her eyes a bit more and began wiping up the wine off of her plate. David looked over at Marcus and noticed his face seemed off.

"What the hell happened?" He asked, knowing something was amiss.

"Oh nothing baby, seriously. Marcus here just developed a special fondness for your mother that he never imagined he could have," she said with a laugh. "It's all good, baby, I promise. Finish eating, love," she finished. David wasn't satisfied and looked at Marcus.

"Listen to your woman," Marcus said with a bite that was not lost on David.

He opted to ignore it when He was again distracted by His mother's laughter. *God, she is so happy,* He thought to Himself.

"David, uhhh, why don't you step outside with me for a second. I just want a few words with you, nothing major, if that's OK with your lady, of course," Marcus said, attempting as sincere a look as he could muster.

David looked at Marcus skeptically, but agreed to join him. The two men excused themselves and walked outside and stood on the front porch. Marcus retrieved a cigarette from the box in his pocket and lit it, inhaling deeply. He glanced over at David.

"Did Nicole ever tell you about the time she first learned about the other uses for rice?" Marcus began. David sucked His teeth and turned to go back into the house. Marcus stopped Him. "No, no, this is good. Let me tell this story." Marcus lowered his voice a bit.

"You see, I was at a new site and I'd pulled a 14 hours day. Man was I exhausted. I called Nicole during lunch and told her that I'd be in late. She knew that she should have had my dinner waiting for me, right? I mean, that's what any decent woman does for a man who works a long, hard day. Well," he continued, as a sardonic smile spread across his face, "I came home and didn't smell a single thing cooked. Man! Can you believe that shit?" He took another pull from his cigarette, waited a few seconds, then exhaled.

"Came in and found her asleep on the couch, fully clothed, knowing damned well no clothes were allowed in the house. I mean, what the fuck man, right? So I yanked her up out of her sleep and shook her until she awakened. A few slaps, you know, nothing serious. She woke up and I told her to strip. Since she didn't want to cook my rice, I decided to teach her how it could be used when not on my dinner table. You know how that goes, right *Sir*? I poured the rice out on the floor and made the bitch kneel on that rice, right then and there. Made her stay her ass there for an hour while I cooked my own goddamned dinner. Man I was so pissed at her! What man works all day and has to come home and cook his own fucking dinner, right?" Marcus took another drag from his cigarette, shaking his head.

"Man to man, Sir to Sir, be real with me... You ever have those problems with her?" he asked David.

"What was THAT??!?!" Janice yelled as she heard a crash come from the front porch. She and Nicole were running to the front door to see what caused the commotion. Nicole made it first and saw Marcus on his back, David on top of him punching him repeatedly.

"Baby... No!!!" she screamed and ran to try and pull David off of Marcus.

"Oh my God, David what are you DOING?!" Janice yelled. "You're gonna kill that boy!!"

"My boy ain't no punk!" Joseph said from right behind her. He leaned over to see what was going on. "It was bound to happen. Sometimes you gotta let them boys fight it out!"

"Joe, help them!!" she implored.

"A man's gotta fight, Janice!!" he repeated and backed up a few steps, pulling her with him.

"Baby, please, pleeeease you're gonna kill him, baby stop!!" Nicole begged pulling at David's arm.

In the split second she distracted Him, Marcus was able to get a solid punch to David's gut, knocking the wind out of Him. David toppled backwards and He fell into Nicole's legs and she lost her footing. Before she could grab onto anything or anyone, she fell backwards off of the porch screaming, a full flight of steps above the concrete ground. Her body hit the ground with a thud and her head bounced on the concrete at last three times.

"Star!!!" David screamed, shoving Marcus off of Him as He ran down the stairs. "Call an ambulance!!!!" He screamed as He began to see blood trickle onto the ground.

"Nicole, baby...baby wake up, baby please!" He begged. She didn't respond, though she was still breathing. "Call a fucking ambulance!!" He screamed as the tears sprang to His eyes. "Baby please, I'm so sorry, please baby, pleeease don't leave me," He plead as He gathered her body into His arms. He began rocking her back and forth.

Marcus came running down the stairs. "The ambulance is on its way," he assured. "Shit, man, is she OK?" he asked trying to get a better look at her.

"Stay back, motherfucker!! You stay the fuck away from us. This is YOUR fault!! I swear to God if anything happens to her..." He stopped short when He heard the ambulance sirens in the distance. He turned His attention back to Nicole.

"Baby, they're coming. Star, stay with me, they're coming," He said rocking her. "I'm gonna take care of you, baby, I promise. I promise..." He whispered into her hair, blood trickling onto His shirt sleeve.

He could hear Janice's screams and DJ's cries in the background but began to tune them out. All He needed to hear was her heartbeat, and He felt it. He leaned His ear down to her chest and listened to her heart still beating rapidly.

I hear you.

LOVE IS A STAR

9/11/2010 12:55 p.m.

From: GoliathSlayer77

To: LaFemmeNickita

Good afternoon, lady. Allow me the pleasure of making your acquaintance. I read a few of your posts in the KOC group and wanted to reach out and let you know that I love your mind, or at least what thoughts I've read so far. I read your profile and am definitely intrigued by the way you articulate your thoughts and present yourself. I'd be lying if I said I didn't enjoy your photos too, lol. You're quite lovely.

I noticed your profile says you're dating, but uncollared. I hope I'm not stepping on any toes or disrespecting anyone with this message. I have no problem respecting boundaries. If you're available, however, I'd love the opportunity to get to know you and maybe make a new friend.

Best,
GS77

9/15/2010 8:35 p.m.

From: LaFemmeNickita

To: GoliathSlayer77

Hello!

I'm sorry for the delay in response. I haven't been online in about a week. I usually take some personal time around 9/11 (lost my dad in the Towers) and head to New York City with my mother and sister. I appreciate your message and your approach was welcomed. You'd be surprised how many lame introductions I get. "What up, boo?" doesn't quite work for me, yanno? Lol.

You're correct, I'm currently uncollared. I'm also single, but I do date when I have time and when someone sparks my interest, which I find is becoming less frequent these days. You're not stepping on any toes at all, and I thank you for that consideration.

So what do you want to know, Mr. Slayer?

-Nick

9/17/2010 5:35 a.m.

From: GoliathSlayer77

To: LaFemmeNickita

Good morning Nick!

I hope this message finds you well. I'm glad you got back to me. I admit I was getting a bit worried. My condolences to you and your family. I lost a couple of colleagues on 9/11 myself. It was just terrible. Can you believe it has been 9 yrs already? Time flies, but that doesn't mean it gets any easier.

I'm a bit of a traveler myself, so I understand time limitation. I get it, definitely. In fact, I'm at the airport now on my way home from a business trip.

What do I want to know? Is "everything" too much? Lol. Maybe we can start with why you're on a site for kinksters and whether or not you're seeking to build with someone? I see you identify as a "sub", but not a "slave". Maybe you can elaborate on that?

Full disclosure: I'm rather new to The Life. I've experimented with some edgier things intimately, but haven't felt fulfilled in my past relationships and interactions beyond that. I want to explore the side of me that I feel remains dormant. Not sure how I can best go about that, but I'm hoping to connect with folks here who can maybe offer some guidance.

Hope to hear from you soon,

David

9/17/2010 4: 43 p.m.

From: LaFemmeNickita

To: GoliathSlayer77

Ahhh David. I get it! Goliath Slayer. Cute! My name is Nicole, and I go by Nickita here. They once knew me in The Life as "Luna", but that's another story, maybe I'll tell you one day. I'm on the site because I enjoy the community aspect of it. It's difficult to find kinksters offline because people aren't always "out" with their kink, if you know what I mean. The site gives me the chance to learn more about what it is that we do, meet other people in The Life, connect with people with more experience, help those with less, etc. I really enjoy the conversations we have on various kink-related topics, especially those related to POC. You know that, though, because that's how you found me ^_^

Hmmm. Yes I definitely identify as a sub, but not slave. Not because I've not considered it or have any particular aversion to the label, as some of "us" do. Just that I only reached that level of service once and it wasn't...good. Let's just say that... It would take a whole lot for me to get close to that place again. At least that's what I tell myself, for now.

I don't call myself submissive because I don't have a submissive personality, not exactly. I'm a rather dominant woman in my vanilla life. I do, however, crave the dominance of a strong man who knows how to take control of His sub and their relationship. I'm also drawn to sadists lol Yes, I'm a bit of a pain slut, as they say. I'm into pushing my personal limits to achieve ultimate pleasure so long as it is with someone I trust and feel comfortable with. I tend to prefer High Protocol dynamics, as I find the structure best suits my kink and fetish needs. That, of course, requires a man who is capable of reigning in my sometimes wild ways *smile*

You're a newbie though, so I don't know... You might not be well-versed in that type of thing. I also noticed you're younger than I am. What draws your to older women? Or was it just me?

Peace,

Nick

P.S. I've been spending less time on here, so can we switch to email? Hit me up at LaFemmeNickita46@gmail.com

9/17/2010 8:13 p.m.

From: "David E. Woods" <david.e.woods77@gmail.com>

To: "LaFemmeNickita46@gmail.com" <LaFemmeNickita46@gmail.com>

Subj: One Step Closer...

Good evening Nicole,

Thank you for inviting me one step closer to you. I'm honored you trust me with your email address. I know there are a lot of weirdos out there, so it's risky.

So, what's a lovely woman like you doing on a Friday night? I'm sure you're out and about or on your way out. You seem like you keep a full social calendar. Well, at least you seem like the kind of woman people would want to be around often.

Yes, I'm new, but not a novice. I'm a grown man! LOL. I don't think 33 is a "young man". Well, maybe in The Life. I think I see what you mean ;) I might not be well-versed in the history and literature of the BDSM lifestyle from de Sade to Black Orpheus, but I know a few things. Particularly, I know how to handle women. I am well-equipped with what is needed to guide women, provide for them, and own them. Women like you are my preference, actually. You're not a challenge per se, but you know what you want out of life and that makes my job that much easier. All I have to do is make sure you do your best to get it and do so according to what I deem is the best for you.

Got it?

Yeah. It's like that.

-David

9/17/2010 10:43 p.m.

From: "Nicole White" <LaFemmeNickita46@gmail.com>

To: "David E. Woods" <david.e.woods77@gmail.com>

Subj: Re: One Step Closer...

Good evening Mr. Woods,

It's like that? Hmmm. We'll see. We shall definitely see.

I'm just getting in, actually. Went to get some drinks with some of my girlfriends. We try to get together at least once a month when our schedules can line up. It's becoming increasingly difficult to do so these days. I'm a little tipsy lol

I think I'm going to just catch the repeat of Bill Maher before I pass out. What about you? What are you up to?

-Nick

P.s. When are you going to let me see what you look like? You didn't have any pictures posted on the site. You hiding from someone? You married? What's the deal?

9/17/2010 10:52 p.m.

From: "David E. Woods" <david.e.woods77@gmail.com>

To: "LaFemmeNickita46@gmail.com" <LaFemmeNickita46@gmail.com>

Subj: Re: One Step Closer...

I like the way "Mr. Woods" reads coming from you. We'll stick with that for now. I'm attaching a picture. I don't have anything to hide, not really. I just don't put myself out there like that. I prefer my privacy. I'm not like you, superstar! And yes, I've seen you around other places online, so I'm up on what you're about. I read some of your blogs the last time I was in the air. You are definitely a fascinating woman. I appreciate how expository you are.

You watch Bill? I love that show. He really doesn't give a fuck does he? It cracks me up when he shits on his guests. I think I'll join you in watching that.

And, you can respond via g-chat. I see you are logged on.

-D

10:56 p.m.

Hello Mr. Woods

Hello Nicole

So here we are

Indeed. Here we are.

You're gorgeous.

Do you drink at all?

Every now and then. I tend to stay away from the stuff for the most part. And thank you :)

May I ask why?

You may ask.

Why do you stay away from alcohol, Mr. Woods?

My dad has had some issues with alcoholism. It's done a number on my family over the years, so I don't want to follow in his footsteps, if that makes sense.

It does. I'm sorry to hear that.

Not your fault

I know. Still... I work with substance abusers, so... I know the impact of alcoholism and drug abuse on families.

That's noble of you. Why did you choose that line of work?

I guess it chose me. I just feel like I was put here to help people.

You think you could help me?

With what do you need help, Mr. Woods?

I want to grow, Nicole. It's hard to explain. Or maybe to you it isn't. I want to grow into the man I know I can be. The man I know I am. The man that people might not understand, you know?

I know. I get it.

I find myself so frustrated sometimes, with no outlet. Knowing that there exists, within me, an insatiable hunger for things that don't make much sense, that I should know and accept are wrong, that I should deny myself.

You're not wrong.

How do I know that?

If you're wrong, then I'm wrong. I'm rarely wrong lol

Is that right?

Yup! :P

A brat. I see...

That's what they say. I just think I'm cute.

You are. You're also beautiful, sexy, and intriguingly captivating.

Well thank you, Sir.

Shit, I'm sorry... Mr. Woods

Either is fine. You know it, as do I.

Noted.

What are you wearing, Nicole?

White robe. You?

Show me.

Now?

Nicole... Do not make me repeat myself.

Ok. Hold on.

How do you want to see? Webcam? Emailed photo?

MMS. 267-555-9846

Hold on.

Last message sent 11:17 p.m.

David's Status Message: Captivated.

Sent.

Received. Lovely. Your pout...is going to prove problematic.

I wasn't pouting!

No, you weren't, but it's there, behind the facade. There is a hint in the way your lips seem to quiver in the picture. You're a pouter. A pouty brat. We'll work on that.

I am not!

You're pouting now.

Aren't you?

Nfdsjfs;fdbdsvbdsjvbsd;vs

What was that? I couldn't hear you over the keyboard smash and through the pouting lol

Look at you acting like you know me.

I will know you. Believe that.

So, do I get to see what you're wearing?

No.

Why not?

Because you don't yet know that you will not be questioning me, that's why.

......

Fix your face, woman.

Fine.

Lol. This is going to be fun.

What is?

Again with the questioning. Tsk tsk tsk.

Sir...

Bedtime for you, Nicole. We'll talk in the morning.

David E. Woods is offline.

****

Conversation with Mr. Woods

10/31/10 8:30 a.m.

Good Morning, Mr. Woods. Are we still on for this evening?

Good morning, Nicole. Yes, we are. I touch down in Philly at 6. You're arriving at 5:45, right?

Yes, Sir. That's correct. Want to meet at 30th street station?

No, the hotel is fine. I don't want to risk delays and have you waiting. I reserved the room in your name to be safe. Don't worry about leaving a card for incidentals; I've taken care of that

Ok. Sounds good. I'm excited to finally meet you! Finally we can get our scheduled to work out, right?

Yeah. It's been tough. I was beginning to think you were avoiding me.

Why would I do that?

Who knows? You know how these internet things can be. Folks fake out a lot. You might be a faker.

You really believe that?

Nah, I'm just fucking with you lol. Plus, I've seen you on camera. I've seen you be nasty on camera. LOL.

There YOU go smh

I may go, but you sure came. Yes, indeed.

So did you. So...

We're not talking about me, though. Are you wearing what I requested?

Yes, I am. Red blouse, black skirt, red heels, hair down. It's the first Halloween in a LONG time that I'm not going out in costume.

You must be special. At least it's Monday and not a Saturday night.

I am special. If I weren't, you wouldn't be meeting me tonight. Good. I look forward to seeing you draped in red in person. I bet it looks great against your skin.

Red does go well on my skin

Are we still discussing clothing, Nicole?

Hmmmm.

I asked you a question. Answer me.

No, Mr. Woods, we're not still discussing clothing.

To what were you referring, then?

Red marks, welts, bruises...

Do you enjoy receiving those, Nicole? I imagine they look divine on you. I hope to adorn you with my own... jewelry... at some point.

It would be an honor to be so adorned, Sir.

As long as you recognize that. Meeting. Talk soon.

11/1/2010 11:17 p.m.

From: "Nicole White" <LaFemmeNickita46@gmail.com>

To: "David E. Woods" <david.e.woods77@gmail.com>

Subj: Home

Good evening, Sir.

Writing to let you know I'm home, as instructed.

You asked me to outline three things that I hope to achieve during my training which is to begin in 3 months. I had time to reflect upon them on the way home, a bit. Here goes:

1. Above all, I want to learn how best to serve you. I want to learn your needs and your wants and make sure they're fulfilled at all times. I don't ever want there to be any voids in your life that I could have filled had I been more in tune with what you were seeking from me.

2. I want to push the envelope of my pain threshold. I want to build with you in such a way that I trust you to help me dig deeper into my craving for it and how I am able to manage it.

3. I want to be trained in complete surrender and submission. I want you to guide me in that journey and provide me with the help and tools I need mentally, physically, and emotionally to do so.

If you require further elaboration, please let me know.

Good night,

Nicole

Conversation with Mr. Woods

11/1/10 11:38 pm

Good girl. Miss you. Sleep well.

****

11/2/2010 3:37 a.m.

From: "David E. Woods" <david.e.woods77@gmail.com>

To: "LaFemmeNickita46@gmail.com" <LaFemmeNickita46@gmail.com>

Subj: Sleepless...

What have you done to me, woman?

I'm sitting up in my bed writing this email, trying to work through things that I don't fully understand.

Who are you?

Why are you here?

Why did you come into my life now? In the way that you have?

I watched you walk into the hotel and found myself struggling to breathe. I coughed, not realizing I was holding my breath. My God, woman, you are insanely beautiful. I saw you before, but I was able to truly see you. Your walk is hypnotic, your stride so confident and sexy. I looked around and the other men noticed it too and something in me almost snapped. I wanted to rip their heads off for ogling you that way. The way I was. I felt immediate possession and protection of you. I was experiencing a revelation of some powerful Truth that I'd never been told and it was you.

I silently watched you check in, flashing that smile I'd seen so many times in various pictures and on camera, but it was brighter then. You were glowing and I was so drawn to your light, I wanted to run over to you like moth to a flame. It was so hard keeping my cool.

Damn girl.

I scared the shit out of you when I came up behind you at the elevator, didn't I? LOL Your expression was priceless. Glad I caught your bag for you. You should know that I have great reflexes and my reaction time is impeccable. You can trust in that. You recognized me after a few seconds and embraced me, without hesitation. I could feel your comfort with me. I can tell the difference. You melted into me. You seemed to breathe me in for a minute. Was that so? Were you breathing me in? Your eyes were closed. Your eye shadow was nice. I love how you do your make up. You don't need it though. I'm not just saying that. I know you feel more comfortable with it, but we'll work on that.

Your lips.

You have the softest lips I've ever kissed. You're a fantastic kisser! I knew you would be, but I just wanted to say that. I don't know why I'm going on rambling and such, but I just have to get this out.

I loved how easy our conversation flowed over dinner, how your genuinely laughed at my jokes, how everything about you is so passionate and real. You are one of the most authentic people I've ever met. It's clear to me that you're sincere in your compassion and you're just... you're just dazzling. That's the word: Dazzling.

And even though you were under no obligation to, you let me have you. You gave yourself to me, openly and freely. Again, without hesitation. You trusted me and believe me, I value the trust you put into me. I was in you and I was inside of you and you welcomed me and for that I thank you.

You could have warned me that you might ruin the sheets, yanno. No, you didn't tell me that you were a squirter. I had to suppress a laugh. I'm really a 12 year old boy inside. Ignore me.

Nicole, I don't want you seeing anyone else. I know that I can't make you do that, not just yet. We're building, still, and working up towards that. I'm just making it known that I want your attention, undivided and complete. I will be giving you mine because...shit... the way you moaned my name over and over, when your eyes rolled back into your head, and the scratches you left on my sides... yeah. I'm sold. I was already completely taken by your personality and our budding friendship, but that pussy is amazing. GODDAMMIT!

Ok.

I'm gonna chill.

I want it. I want to own it and you.

-David

11/2/2010 3:49 a.m.

From: "Nicole White" <LaFemmeNickita46@gmail.com>

To: "David E. Woods" <david.e.woods77@gmail.com>

Subj: Re: Sleepless...

You do. Already.

****

Conversation with Mr. Woods

2/14/11 8:35 pm

So how does it feel to be officially in training?

It feels good. It feels right.

Are you wearing your training collar?

Not at the moment. It's still in the box You gave to me earlier at dinner.

Put it on.

Ok, BRB.

Back.

Welcome.

Thank You, Sir :-)

Do you believe in me?

Yes, Sir, I do.

Do you believe in us?

I do. If You don't mind explaining, why do You ask, Sir?

Because I want to make sure that you're as fully prepared for what we're about to get into together as I am. I want this. I need this. You do too.

You know I do.

So I want to make sure that you're not walking into this lightly.

Sir, I need you to understand that I get it. You know this. It's not my first time…This Life… it is essential to me. This is what I'm built for, what feels right for me. I've missed this type of connection.

But it is mine!

I know…

Respect that.

I do.

I'm trying to do this the right way. I want to make sure that we are both fulfilled and that I can take care of you. Of us.

I know, Sir.

Every day, my feelings for you grow stronger and stronger. Today, we took a step towards the life we both want to live, a life we both say we need.

And we will do so and it will be amazing. I trust in You as You trust in me. Sir, we're going to be fine. I'm going to learn everything I need to know to serve You, fully and completely. I'm committing myself to You. Don't fear me, please…

I don't fear you, my Star. I fear failing you as your Sir.

You will not fail me. Sir, You love me.

Says who? ;)

Says You, earlier today, when You gave me my beautiful new training collar.

Touch it.

I'm there.

You are.

I will always be there.

You will.

And you'll be on your knees waiting for me.

As you wish.

Go to bed, Star.

Goodnight, Sir.

David's Status Message: My Bitch-to-be lol

I love you, David.

I know.

*****

2/14/2013

Nicole blinked a few times to focus, but the lights above her were painfully blinding. They hurt. She closed them again. She focused on listening closely for cues, maybe hearing sounds could help her figure out where she was. She could hear a familiar voice singing and she thought she knew the song, but wasn't sure. The voice she knew though. She tried to smile, but her lips felt sore and cracked. *I need my lip butter*, she thought.

"Until the end of time, I'll be there for you... you own my heart my heart and mind, I truly adore you..."

The voice sang and she felt herself warming up. She'd heard that line sung to her several times before, so she felt at least that wherever she was, she was with someone she knew and someone who made her feel good. She licked her lips and smiled.

"Marcus..." she whispered. She wasn't sure if he heard her or not. She hadn't heard herself so she tried again.

"Marcus!" she yelled, or at least she felt like she yelled.

"I need your help!!"

Still, no response. She gave up. She took a few deep breaths and prepared to call out again when she heard voices getting closer. Two men it sounded like. They weren't happy. Maybe they were arguing. *Well whoever it is, somebody better come get me up outta here and get me my lip butter*, she thought to herself.

"Why the fuck are you in here? Today of all days?" David accused Marcus. "How many times do I have to tell you to stay far away from Nicole as possible?? Huh?? It's been weeks and you're *still* not welcomed here!"

"Look, man," Marcus began, "I just wanted to come by and check on her, OK?" Marcus stood still, annoyed that David interrupted his singing. "It's Valentine's Day, man, have a heart."

"I have a heart, you piece of shit, and she is lying there, unconscious on that bed, because of you and your bullshit. Not a day has gone by when I haven't wanted to rip you apart, limb by limb, hair by hair, and cell by fucking cell!" David hissed.

"Whatever, you ain't gonna do shit. I came here to see Nicole, not you," Marcus continued.

He moved closer to Nicole's bed. He was carrying flowers, so he sat the vase down on the night stand beside her and stood calmly by her bedside. "Just give me a minute, man, damn. You don't think I feel terrible about this??"

"You should feel suicidal. Would save me the trouble," David retorted, without taking a step. Something caught His eye and He thought He saw movement come from Nicole's still body. He rushed to the other side of the bed.

"Baby? Baby are you awake?" He grabbed her hand and began massaging it, as He had done countless times in the past weeks, waiting for some sign of life.

"Baby please, please say something, anything. Just grab my hand if you can," He begged.

Nicole squeezed His hand.

"She just squeezed my hand!! Call the nurse, get the doctor in here!! Now!" He yelled at Marcus. Marcus ran out of the room in search for help.

Nicole opened her eyes again, this time feeling better adjusted. She watched as Marcus left the room and tried to call out to him.

"Marcus!!" she yelled. *Where is he going?*

David looked down at Nicole. He stood for a moment.

"Star?"

Nicole tried to move her heard towards the direction she saw Marcus leaving.

"Star??" David asked again. He grabbed her hand and pulled it to His chest. He caressed her face as tears burned his eyes and threatened to spill over. "Baby, it's me. I'm here," He whispered.

Nicole slowly moved her head towards the man holding her hand and touching her face. She stared into attractive, but sad eyes. She felt something, but she wasn't sure what it was, but her stomach fluttered a bit. She blinked a few times, but couldn't place him.

Who is Star?

"So what do you think? You think you're up to going out to a party?"

Nicole looked up from her computer screen and focused on Marcus, who was sitting on the couch flipping through the television stations. She had a headache, something she had gotten used to over the last three months. Almost every day, in the late evening, she developed a dull, but thumping headache behind her left eye and near her left temple. She usually popped a few Advil and it would subside.

This evening, she was so focused on her writing that she barely noticed how fast it crept up on her. She was writing another journal entry on her tablet. Her neurologist suggested that she keep a journal when thoughts came to her, thoughts that might be memories she struggled with understanding. She typed faster than she wrote, so she kept the entries in her tablet, which was password protected: *0214*. She wasn't sure why she chose that number, but it just came to her so she rolled with it. She looked back at her screen.

David. David. David. Who is he, really? Why does Marcus act like he hates him when they claim to be friends? Why does he check on me so often? Is that why Marcus hates him? Is he jealous? Did there exist some sort of tension between them over me? How long have we known David? Is he a childhood friend of Marcus'? Why does smile at me like that? Why is he so nice? I had yet another dream about David. He and I were on a cruise and we were drinking and gambling. I wore a coral dress and sun hat, he work a pale pink button down shirt and grey slacks. We were then standing against the rails and he was behind me, arms wrapped around me. I was...happy...

Nicole began to type again, ignoring Marcus' question.

I was smiling and I felt warm, not from the sun, but from him.

She back-spaced and capitalized the "H" in Him. Then stared again. Why did I do that? She then scrolled up about 9 pages and reread an earlier entry:

Had another dream about David... we were lying on the floor of my kitchen, crying...

"Nicole?!" Marcus called her name louder, with a more edgy demand. He turned around, wondering what had her distracted. He saw her staring at her tablet intently.

"Hey, baby, don't stare too hard. You might hurt yourself," he cautioned with a half-chuckle.

He stood up and began walking over to her. Nicole closed the document and turned the tablet's screen off. Marcus paused but said nothing. He didn't want to push her...yet. When she woke up in the hospital, she connected with him, to his surprise. He wasn't sure what to do and he definitely wasn't prepared for how she reached out for him and called his name when she fully came to. He loved the look of pure anguish that crossed David's face when it happened, though. He relished that, in fact.

He won.

According to her doctors, Nicole needed as much support as possible by the people she was closest to and she needed to be in familiar company, locations, and the like. They insisted that her amnesia was partial and likely temporary, but there was no telling if she'd ever fully recover her memories or if she did, when that would happen. He and David were cautioned not to push too hard to force her memory to return.

Since Nicole's most recent memories included Marcus being her lover, Marcus happily and eagerly volunteered to help her ease back into her life and recover. David was livid, but He eventually agreed with what the doctors recommended would be the best course of action to help her fully recover. He vowed to stay close, but He would also give her the space needed to avoid or at least minimize confusion.

Before she was released, David went to their apartment and cleaned out His things, moving Himself temporarily into a sublet a few miles away. One of her doctors said she would benefit from picking up life where her last memory left off and since she was focused on Marcus, David's presence might do more harm than good.

He still had keys, though.

David was hopeful that maybe she'd find the lease on her own and see both of their names on it. Maybe she'd find the journal He happened to leave in the drawer of the nightstand by His side of the bed. He also slid her engagement ring into a box with her collars and other adornments He'd gotten her over the years and hid it in the back of her closet. He rationalized to Himself that these subtle hints would be helpful in bringing back her memory and that He wasn't being pushy, just helpful.

"Do you want to go out to a party or something? Maybe have some fun? You've been kinda hiding out here for months now. We should go out and get acquainted with our old life. You don't even know what you're missing, baby!" Marcus said.

"I'm not really up to any partying, Marcus," Nicole replied.

"I'm just trying to help, baby girl," Marcus insisted. "Let me take you out so we can have some fun. You still have that freak edge in you that I've always loved. A little bump on the head didn't rob you of that," he said with a genuine laugh this time.

He ran his fingers through her hair and yanked her head back, descending down for a deep kiss. Nicole returned his kiss because she felt like she was supposed to. When he bit her lip, she winced and pulled back, staring at him.

"Too much?" he asked, searching her face for an answer.

"I don't...like that," she answered. "It doesn't seem right. Maybe I liked it before, but I don't now. Please don't bite my lips anymore, Marcus," she asserted.

"OK OK OK," Marcus said, stepping back with hands raised. "I won't bite your lips anymore. My bad, baby. I just know you used to love when I did that, especially when I drew blood. You've always loved my pain," Marcus said, eyes darkening at his own memories.

"Well, I don't now," Nicole confirmed as she stood up and headed to her bedroom to put her tablet away and change into her gym clothes.

She'd made evening trips to the gym part of her new routine. She knew she was into working out; it felt routine to her. She remembered growing up heavy and she felt compelled to work out, so she did what came naturally. David mentioned that He recalled her being a member of a gym about three blocks away from her house and sure enough, she saw the membership card on her key chain. Marcus knew nothing about that.

After the accident, Nicole was let go from her job, as they claimed they weren't obligated to hold her job for longer than 8 weeks. Rather than fill her position with a temporary worker, they opted to hire someone new, so Nicole no longer had much to do during the day. She wasn't even aware of her position or the agency for which she worked, but they did give her a year's salary as severance, so she was financially comfortable for a while. She could not bring herself to look for work because she still struggled daily feeling like pieces of her were missing. She knew she wanted to help people, somehow.

Marcus told her she was a social work administrator, so that feeling of wanting to help others made sense. She could not help others, however, until she helped herself. She knew Marcus. Marcus felt normal. Normal didn't exactly feel right, though, and Nicole could not understand why she felt unsettled and occasionally fearful when she was around him. Marcus was her man and she felt like she was supposed to love him. Maybe she'd forgotten what love was too? Both Marcus and David refused to answer her when she prodded for details about what happened to her before she fell into a coma. They both gave the same answer, "The doctors think its best you not know the details until they come back to you."

Great.

She knew how to cook. She found herself spending more and more time in her kitchen, coming up with new recipes and concoctions. Her house felt empty, like something or someone was missing. She asked Marcus if they lived together, because she said she felt a masculine presence, but he said they didn't, that they did once.

His name wasn't in her phone.

He couldn't explain that.

Nicole finished getting dressed and went back into the living room. She thought Marcus would have taken the hint that it was time for him to leave, but he seemed even more comfortable on her couch than before.

"Marcus, I'm headed to the gym. When I get back, I'm gonna head to bed. I'm pretty tired as it is," she told him.

"Why not just stay in and rest? We could watch your show, Scandal. Baby girl you know you love you some Olivia Pope. It's all up in your DVR," he chided, laughing.

"I don't know... I watched a few episodes and... I don't get it. Like, she went from being a teen mom saving the last dance to being a Republican side chick? I just don't get it..."

"You women love that show!"

"Maybe I did, but I don't see the appeal now. And what's up with Harrison? Where are his balls? Who wrote out his manhood? Blah!"

"True. He is kind of bitchassed."

"Hey!" Nicole said, chuckling. "Don't be so harsh!" She laughed because she thought the same thing watching the last episode. She shook her head and grabbed her keys.

"Well, you gotta go," she said plainly.

Marcus sighed and stood up. "Fine. Fine. Fiiiiine. I'll go. Enjoy your workout. I'll call you later and check on you."

"No, you don't have to. I'm good," Nicole said, opening the front door. Marcus followed behind her.

As she locked the door, she continued, "You know, you really don't have to check on me so much. I'm fine, really. I've been really focusing on writing down my memories and I feel like I've been making progress. I can focus more when I have some space."

"So what are you saying?"

"I'm saying that I need some space, Marcus."

"What does space mean? What do you want?"

"I'm asking you to give me some time to myself. I have a lot of things to work on and figure out."

"So when should I call you?"

Nicole paused and slowly turned to face him and look him in the eyes.

"Marcus, I'll call you. Ok?"

"Fine."

Marcus didn't wait for the elevator, instead opting to take the stairs. When the door to the stairwell closed behind him, Nicole breathed a sigh of relief. She felt like she finally exhaled breath she had been holding in for three months. She pushed the elevator button realizing that would be the last time she would see Marcus for a while.

****

David parked His car in the parking lot of Nicole's gym. He decided to get a membership last week when He realized that He could not remain passive anymore. He had given Nicole three months to adjust to her surroundings and He felt that was more than enough time. He was suffering tremendously, in every aspect of His life, and He could not take it anymore.

He needed His woman back.

He had to take some time off from work because He found Himself completely distracted by everything that had happened. He explained to his supervisor what was going on and she understood Hid pain, having met Nicole several times. She referred Him to their Employee Assistance Program and the contact there got Him connected with a therapist that He starting meeting with every other week. After the first three sessions, His therapist recommended that He go on vacation and get away from His daily routine for a while, so He went away to clear His head a bit.

He wanted to check on His father, but could not reach him, and He didn't bother looking for him. He found a quaint Bed & Breakfast in New Jersey, run by a pleasant lesbian couple that could cook their behinds off. They were open to Him and took good care of Him for the week, even gave Him two nights free. He tipped them the cost of the two nights instead, because He realized that week saved His sanity.

Fuck Marcus. If he so much as touches my Star, I'm going to kill his ass.

In the weeks immediately following Nicole's release from the hospital, David was consumed with thoughts of Marcus taking advantage of Nicole's memory loss and violating her. He had nightmares of him assaulting her and her calling out for Him to save her. He would wake up, covered in sweat, and grab His phone to call her... then put the phone away. He could not disturb her. She would not understand.

Instead, He decided to make Himself more present in her life and maybe, over time, she would come to remember Him. He told Himself that he would not press her. He would simply be there. Wherever she was, He would be there.

He felt like a complete creep.

He knew this was around the time she came to the gym so He knew to be there at this time. He got out of His car and walked towards the entrance. He saw her coming down the street, so He slowed His pace. He stared at Her, briefly, before she would notice His gaze. He absorbed her.

God, she's beautiful. My baby...

He breathed deep and when she got closer, He opened the door. She looked up to thank Him and recognized Him, greeting Him with a warm smile.

"Hey Star," He said, instinctively.

"Good evening, Sir," Nicole responded, nodding her head in His direction.

David paused for a moment and stared at her. He wanted to lean in and kiss her forehead, but refrained. *Did she...?*

"What's up?" she asked, cheerily. "You work out here too? I didn't know that! How come I've never seen you here before?"

"Eh, I just joined last week," He began, disappointed. "My gym is getting too crowded and you always raved about how much better your gym was than mine, so…"

"I did? Well, it is pretty awesome. Come on in, let me see what you're working with," she said, playfully punching him in the ribs. David wanted to grab her hand and put it on His hardening penis, but restrained himself.

Goddammit, woman.

****

"Who are we?? What we run? The worrrrrrlddddddddd!! Who run this mutha unh unh!!"

Nicole was finishing up her 3-miles run on the treadmill. David looked over at her screen, then back at His, with its paltry 1.25 miles and shrugged. He was tired. Dead tired. She'd gotten fast during her recovery time. She was darling, though, singing along with Beyoncé while she ran. They were almost done. David was thinking about how He could make His way back to their apartment. He had to be smooth with His approach.

"Hey! You wanna come over for a bit and maybe have some coffee??!!" Nicole yelled, trying to speak over the music in her headphones.

David leaned over and pulled her earbud out of her left ear. "Yes," He said with a smile. "I'd love to. I've wanted to catch up with you, but… Marcus… you know…"

"Yeah, well," Nicole said in between deep breaths, "I told Marcus I needed some space. I'm still trying to figure things out and I feel like he is crowding me a bit. Does that make sense? Ugh I shouldn't be telling you that."

David turned off his treadmill. "No no no, it's totally fine. I get it. I can't imagine he's given you much time to yourself. He seems pretty overprotective."

"For real," she said, turning off her own treadmill. "I feel like I haven't had a moment to myself to do anything. So, I asked him to kinda back up a bit and let me breathe," she said with a dramatic eye roll.

They cleaned off their machines and left the gym, walking towards their apartment.

"Come on, it's this way, only a few blocks," Nicole said.

"I know, Nicole," David said quietly and followed her to the apartment. They walked silently, each winding down from the workout and focusing on their breathing. One of the things they enjoyed most about each other was that they had perfected the ability to sustain companionable silence. They never felt the need to force conversation or fill the space between them. It was not empty space. It was a space where that which existed beyond love flowed between them. It came naturally in this moment. David remembered it well and hoped Nicole recognized it.

When they got to the building, Nicole told David that she needed to shower and He told her He would make Himself comfortable. She offered Him a towel and washcloth so He could shower too.

"What am I supposed to wear when I'm done? My sweaty clothes?"

"I found some men's clothing in my closet a while back. I can iron those for you, if you'd like," Nicole answered.

David felt Himself begin to stir.

"Oh, you don't have to. I'll be ok..."

"Oh no no no, Sir," she said playfully. "You're a guest in my home. Let me take care of you," she continued, curtseying in front of Him.

"Stop that," David said, half-serious. She had no idea what her supplication was doing to Him.

Nicole shook her head, "Fiiine!" She went into the bathroom to take her shower.

David made His way to their bedroom.

He didn't have a lot of time.

****

Nicole wrapped her towel around herself. *Shoot, I don't have anything to put on.* She should have been more concerned about being indecent around David, but she felt abnormally comfortable. She actually felt like she was too covered up. *That's odd* she thought to herself. She shrugged it off and dried herself off thoroughly.

"David?" she called out, "Can you please hand me the bathrobe hanging on the door to my closet in my bedroom?"

David did not respond and she wondered if He had heard her.

"David?? Did you hear me?" she asked again, a bit louder this time.

Silence.

Did He leave? What the hell? She opened the bathroom door and went towards her bedroom. She walked in to see David standing in the middle of the open space by her bed. His hands were behind his back. He had lit a candle while she was in the bathroom.

"David, what is going on? What are you–"

"Quiet."

"Excuse me?"

David raised His eyes to stare at her. Nicole met His stare, a questioning look on her face.

"I do not repeat myself Nicole. You know that."

"What the hell are you–"

Nicole could not finish her sentence because in less than two seconds, David had crossed the space between them and had His right hand around her throat. One second later, His left hand pulled her towel off of her body, leaving her completely naked in front of Him. He pushed her back against the wall behind her. She raised her hands to fight Him off, but He grabbed both of her arms with His free hand and pushed them over her head behind her, pinning them against the wall. His right hand squeezed a bit tighter around her throat.

"Baby...how do I look?"
"You look beautiful, Star."
"Well, you would say that since you picked this outfit out!"
"I wasn't talking about the outfit. I was talking about you."
"Aww baby, you're so sweet..."

"You... are... mine..." He growled into her right ear before His mouth descended onto her shoulder, kissing it first then biting. Nicole twisted her body in an instinctual fight against His attack, then tried to raise her feet to kick her feet up, but He spread her feet wide, trapping them with His. She could not move.

She was His. In that moment, she was His...again.

David felt a tear release itself and fall to her shoulder. He kissed it.

"You see that star right there?"
"Which one, Sir?"
"That one, riiiight there"
"Mmhmmm, I see it"
"See how bright it's shining?"
"Mmhmmm"
"That's you, Star. You shine so bright in my life."
"You say the nicest things, Sir"
"I adore you."

"Remember me..."

He whispered, tightening His hand around her throat as He felt her resistance waning. He glanced at her out of the corner of His eye. She was still with Him. She was not about to faint. He knew her, knew her threshold. She could handle way more than this.

"You're not letting me walk away, are you?"
"No."
"I didn't think so."
"But you have to tell me if you want to. Tell me if you're unhappy, Star."
"If I am unhappy, You will fix it. We will make it better."
"I want you to know that you can leave if you have to."
"Do you mean that?"
"No."
"I didn't think so."

"Know me..."

He felt her arms give up their fight and He released His hold on them. They fell around His neck. His right hand eased its grip on her throat and He felt her shaking her head. He looked back at her and saw her lips moving.

"More..." she managed to get out, a crack in her whisper.

He tightened His grip on her throat as His left hand traveled lower to feel out her response. She was drenched. She was preparing herself for Him, despite every memory her mind lost. Her body remembered and responded. He clasped her wetness, gently at first, then more firmly.

"Mine!" He muttered harshly into her ear.

"What did you put in my drink?"
"Ha ha"

"No, seriously, Sir. What the hell happened? When did I fall in love with You?"

"It took a while, but it was bound to happen."

"Mmhmmm."

"I mean, how can I not...?"

"I know"

"You're mine."

"Always."

He lifted her right leg slightly, giving Him enough room to position Himself for entry. He stopped Himself and looked at her.

"Say you want this. Say it!"

"I...want...this..."

"Are you sure, Nicole?"

"Yes...yes... it feels...."

David was inside of her before she could finish her thought. He wrapped first her right leg, then her left leg around His waist. She tightened her grip on His neck as He lifted her and fully positioned her on top of His hardness. He moved within her with the desperation of a starved prisoner of war. He battled internally, feeling He might be taking advantage of her. He slowed down, but then felt her legs wrap around Him tighter.

"Don't stop...don't stop...this is... this is..." she panted.

"This is...what?"

"This is amazing. This is what I've needed. Oh God don't stop, don't stop..."

"Quiet."

Nicole let out a moan.

"Are you here?"

Nicole gasped as she felt Him deep inside of her.

"My Star, are... you... here??!"

"Yes...," her nails dug into His back.

"...Sir."

"Mmmm... Good morning," Nicole said groggily, smiling at David's closed eyes and lips.

He inhaled and exhaled steadily. His eyelid fluttered but remained closed. His chest rose and fell. Nicole traced the outline of His upper lip with her index finger, slowly...deliberately.

"Good morrrrning," she purred, again, trying to awaken Him. She was horny. Really horny.

He opened one eye, slightly, and looked down at her.

"You're speaking to...?"

"You, silly!" she responded, playfully smacking His chest. He grabbed her wrist before she could smack His chest again and squeezed.

"Again...to whom are you speaking?"

Nicole paused with a confused look on her face. She looked down, trying to figure out what she was doing or saying wrong. She felt His hand tighten its grasp on her wrist as her fingers began to throb. In the next moment, David was on top of her, the length of His body covering hers, His weight pressing down, binding her. He pushed her wrist above her head with His left hand and grabbed her other hand with His right, pinning it at her side.

"Sir."

Nicole squirmed under Him, the pressure on her wrists becoming increasingly painful.

"Say it."

"Sir, Sir, Sir!"

David raised His eyebrow. "That's funny to you? Oh, I see."

"No, no, no."

"No...*what?*"

"No, Sir."

"Spread your legs."

She looked into His eyes and was startled by the intensity of His lust. His eyes were darker and there was not one single trace of a smile on His face. He meant business. She kept her legs closed.

"Defiant....bitch," He bit out, annoyed. "Spread your legs, woman."

She arched her back and attempted to stretch her body. His right leg worked its way between hers and forced her legs open. In a swift move, He released her hands, grabbed her hips, and buried Himself deep inside of her welcoming wetness.

She *was* horny.

He slowly and deeply stroked her as she began to open up for Him, completely. The first moan escaped, then a second, louder one. Then her eyes clenched closed and her palms grabbed the sheets. He quickened His pace, beads of sweat forming across His forehead. He raised Himself to His knees, bringing her up with Him so that her hips were elevated off of the bed. He pushed her knees back towards her breasts, as He filled her to capacity with every down stroke. She reached towards His chest, her nails connecting with His nipples. He winced, but kept up His rhythm. She scratched Him again, digging her nails deeper again this time. Again, He winced.

"Stop that."

"Why? Does it hurt?" she asked with a smirk.

She pinched and pulled His left nipple, biting her lip as she enjoyed His jerking reaction.

"Well...does it?"

"You know what that shit does to me," He responded, slowing the pace down a bit. He leaned down, bringing His face closer to hers. "Don't play with me, woman."

"Playing is fun....*Sir*"

Nicole gasped as she felt David's hand around her throat squeezing, cutting off her air supply. He resumed His rapid pace, stroking her deep, hitting her walls as deeply as He could fit.

"Watch your fucking tone, Star."

David closed His eyes, feeling Himself disconnect from the scene somewhat. He was in His zone. His space. Again...

He smacked her mouth for her petulance. Twice to make a point. He faintly heard her muffled vacillation between gasps for life and moans of little deaths. She was still alive. She was fine. He pulled out of her only for as long as it took to turn her over onto her stomach. He spread her cheeks wide and entered her from behind. He glanced down and saw that he was covered in white cream. She loved every moment of His assault. He allowed the space to engulf Him, falling forward onto her. He bit her left ear, then sucked it, then bit it again. She yelped, so He bit harder. She cried out and He smiled.

"Breathe."

She took a deep breath as He turned her head to face into the pillow. His right hand grabbed the back of her neck, pushing her face into the pillow as His left hand grabbed her waist. He continued to pump into her, feeling Himself reach His peak. He knew she would join Him there momentarily.

He let go of her neck and she immediately turned her head to breathe in deeply. Her walls tightened around Him and He knew she was about to explode. He hit her spot, over and over, feeling Himself ready to explode.

"Come with me. Now. NOW!" He commanded. He felt her walls tighten, almost painfully around Him, and felt the gush of her release hot against His skin. This sent Him over the edge and He unleashed His own flow deep into her. He grabbed her close to Him and buried His face between her shoulder blades.

They breathed. Each other. Absorbing the other's existence... in that moment. No words spoken as they recovered and returned to themselves.

"You have a lot to learn...again."

****

"Gah, I have *no* idea what to wear today!"

Nicole brushed her teeth, lamenting her indecisiveness right before such an important interview. Two weeks ago, with David's encouragement, she began sending out her resume to see if it would get any bites. Within a few days, she had lined up three job interviews and two reputable community-based organizations and one philanthropy firm.

The firm's interview was scheduled for that morning and she was nervous because the opportunity was simply amazing. The firm was located in Washington, D.C. and she had already slam-dunked the phone interview. They were highly impressed with her, and since the deputy CEO was in town for a board meeting, she agreed to meet with Nicole in person for a brunch interview.

David walked over to stand in the bathroom doorway. He took a moment to enjoy the view of Nicole standing with a towel around her hips, naked from the waist up, hair pinned atop her head, as she frantically brushed her teeth. He has been back in His home for about a month and still reveled in having His woman back where she belongs. With Him.

"Mine."

"Huh, Baby?"

"Nothing," He said, dismissing His unconscious uttering. "Your suit is pressed and hanging behind the bedroom door."

"It is? Awww thank you!"

"Of course it is. What did you expect?"

David struggled a bit with accepting that there were certain things Nicole was not used to, having been disconnected with her previous well-trained presentation of self. That training took almost two years to get as close to perfection as One might hope for. She understood her connection to Him, though, and her submission resonated deep within her spirit. He knew He could work with that, as that was probably the most important element of their dynamic – the spiritual balance of her submission and His Dominance. The particulars of protocol could be relearned and He knew this would be a test of His patience and endurance. She was absolutely worth it, though, so He made no complaints. He just tried to find the best ways to nudge her back into her 'place' without being overbearing.

Sometimes, though, He just wished she would get it together.

"I always pick out your outfits, Star..." He reminded her quietly.

She stopped brushing, rinsed her mouth out, and walked over to where He stood. She laced her fingers behind His neck and pressed her breasts against His chest.

"I'm trying..." she whispered.

"I know."

"I'll get better."

"I know you will."

"I wish I could hit a reset button and go back before the accident."

He sighed deeply, saying nothing.

"It wasn't your fault, Sir." She stroked the hair at the nape of His neck. "I'm sorry that I disobeyed you that day."

"Don't. It's done. It's over. We're here. You. Me. We're here. I have my baby back," He reassured her, hugging her close to Him. They embraced for a few seconds before Nicole reached down and untucked her towel, letting it fall to the ground.

"On your knees," He whispered into her ear. She slid down and positioned herself on her knees, at His feet, head down.

"This morning, you woke up and made two errors. What were they?"

"I...I didn't call you, Sir. I'm sorry."

"What else?"

She could not, for the life of her, think of what else she might have done wrong. She only knew, in that moment, she could not stand the feeling of being a complete disappointment to her Sir. Her anxiety levels began to rise and she began to tremble.

"Sir, I... I don't know. I don't...."

"Before you utter a single word, you are to remember that your mouth has a greater purpose. Your lips, your tongue exist to please me. As such, your first action is to use your mouth to service me. Do you understand?"

"I think so..."

"You think so?" He grabbed her hair and pulled her head up.

"Look at me!"

She raised her eyes to meet His.

"Give me your hand."

She raised her right hand and He grabbed it and placed it on His full erection.

"Open your mouth"

She opened her mouth and moved towards her hand. She was now focused on tasting Him and realized it had been a while and then....it clicked...

"Oh God, Sir!!! I'm so sorry, so so sorry. I was supposed to wake you up the *right way*."

"Shut up!" He commanded, pushing Himself beyond her parted lips.

"This... is... how... you... will...awaken me...every fucking day... Do you hear me??"

She could offer no response, as He completely occupied her throat.

"Don't ever make me wait this long again, OK??"

She nodded her head and focused on not gagging. She closed her eyes and accepted her current duty and proceeded to take care of her Sir. She placed her hands on His cheeks, caressing and pulling Him closer. She wanted to make up for her transgression.

"Stop, baby. It's all good. We're good. You have to get ready for your interview." He pulled back and helped her stand up. He cupped her face in His hands and kissed her lips, gently.

"You know I love you, right?" she whispered against His lips.

"Yes. You show me every day," He responded.

"I'm going to fix this," she promised.

"We're going to fix this. You're mine," He reminded her.

"All yours. You're mine?" she asked.

"Maybe," He responded with a twinkle in His eyes. "Clearly!" He confirmed.

"Go get dressed," He said, swatting her on her behind. "You better bang this interview out...or else."

"I got this!"

Nicole got dressed and grabbed her valise and car keys. She went downstairs, going over possible interview questions and her responses. She accidentally dropped her keys and reached down to grab them. When she came upright, she accidentally bumped into someone making his way towards her.

"Oh excuse me, I'm sorry!"

"It's quite alright, Beautiful. Be careful," the man said with a smile Nicole could not help but notice and admire.

Damn, He's fine.

She continued towards her car, clicking her remote to open the trunk before she got there. She tossed her valise in, slammed the trunk, and clicked again to open the doors. She rushed around to the driver's side and got in. She put the key in the ignition and adjusted her mirror. She saw the man she just bumped into standing behind her car.

What the hell?

She put her car into reverse and waited for him to move. When he didn't, she honked her horn. "Come on!!" she yelled. "What the fuck are you doing??" The man stood still. Keeping her foot on the brake, Nicole dug into her pocket for her phone to call David. She was startled by a banging on her window and dropped her phone to the car floor.

"You're gonna pay for what you did to Marcus, Bitch!!!" the man's muffled yell promised. Just as quickly as he arrived, the man ran off and Nicole began to shake. She put the car into park and dialed David's number. There was no answer. She dialed again and it rang six times and went to His voicemail answering service. *Why the fuck isn't He answering?? Is He in the shower? Dammit!!*

Nicole took the keys out of the ignition and got out of the car. She looked around and saw no sign of the man anywhere, so she walked as fast as she could in her heels back to her apartment building. She paced as she waited for the elevator and paused when she got to her door.

The door was ajar.

"David??!" she called out. "Baby, I called you. I just had the craziest shit happen in the parking lot!"

She pushed the door open and dropped her phone and keys, gasping at the scene in front of her.

She breathed deeply.

"Marcus... Put... the gun...down. Please..."

"Leave."

David quietly gave His command to a near-paralyzed Nicole. Keeping His eyes locked with Marcus', He made no move other than to part His lips. He stood by their over-sized brown loveseat, His pale blue-and-white striped business shirt half buttoned with a cerulean tie hanging loosely over His shoulders. He wore boxer-briefs and trouser socks, as He had not yet put on His slacks.

Marcus stood in the foyer by their dining room, his back to Nicole. His broad shoulders heaved as he breathed deeply and rapidly, his shaky right hand pointing a compact 9mm Beretta pistol towards David's head.

"No, don't leave, baby girl. You're just in time. Yeah, just in time to see what a punk assed bitch your man really is," he asserted.

"Marcus! What are you d--?!"

"Did you not hear me, woman??" David interrupted, His voice slightly betraying His urgency. He chanced a glance at her and caught her eye. He stared for a couple of seconds, hoping she got the message that He wanted her to leave before things escalated further.

"You're fucking crazy!!!" she condemned.

Of course she didn't.

"You still don't have your bitch under control, huh?" Marcus taunted, laughing. "You would think that bump on the head might have knocked some sense into her." He turned his head to the left, keeping his right arm extended towards David.

"Come here, bitch."

Nicole would not move. Could not move. She looked to David for guidance, but His eyes were locked on Marcus again, His focus narrowing on the pistol gripped in Marcus' palm.

I can't leave Him.

She took a hesitant step towards Marcus, then another. By the third, Marcus grabbed her arm and pulled her against him, wrapping his forearm around her neck. She yelped and tried to pry his arm away. David flinched forward.

"Unh unh! Stay back, muthafucka, before I put a bullet in her and make you watch her die... for real this time."

"You hurt her and I promise you, on everything I hold sacred, I will delight in your suffering."

"Tough words for a man without a gun..."

"Weak moves for a boy with one."

Marcus squeezed his arm tighter around Nicole's neck, barely noticing her grabbing and clawing at his flesh. David took a step closer to them.

"One more fucking step and I will snap her neck!"

"No... you won't."

"Fuck you mean, I won't?? You telling me what I'mma do, bitch? Huh?"

"You won't hurt her," David reiterated. "You won't do anything to her because... you love her. That's why you're here, right now, in this very moment. You're in *my* home, pointing a gun at *my* head like some worthless thug off the street because... you...love...her."

Nicole slowed her flailing and fighting and did the best she could to turn towards David. She felt Marcus' grip loosen a fraction, but she was still trapped behind his massive forearm. David chanced half a step.

"When she was with you, you treated her like everything you feared and knew you didn't deserve. You took advantage of her devotion and innocence. You used her heart and her body, selfishly. You...abused"

"I never abused her! You don't know shit about what *we* had, ain't that right baby girl? Tell him. Tell him I was good to you!" Marcus emphasized his last demand by tightening his arm around Nicole, tighter than before. She choked out a coughing gag.

"You abused her and beat down her spirit," David continued, His words coming to Him a bit easier. He knew He had hit the right nerve. "You took the most delicate of flowers and crumbled its petals. You made it harder for me, sure... but eventually, our love was stronger than anything you ever did to her. And now...you're mad. You're mad, hurt, frustrated, lonely, and... worthless."

"Oh you think you have it all figured out?" Marcus asked, lowering the gun a few inches but keeping it pointed at David. "You don't know shit!"

****

"Come on, baby. You've spent $40 at this booth already. You could have bought me a stuffed animal at a store by now," Nicole said with a laugh. Marcus slapped down another $5 and received 5 balls from the teenager running the game booth at the state fair. He unbuttoned his cuffs and rolled up his sleeves a bit.

"It's the principle, girl."

"What principle? That you enjoy wasting money?"

"That I can knock those bottles down."

"I saw a documentary on how they rig these things, making them almost impossible to win. They do it to get your money from you and"

"I don't give a shit, I'm going to win this. Don't you have faith in me, baby girl?"

"I do, but..."

"There is no 'but'. You either believe in me or you don't."

"I do."

"Good," he said, with a wink. He picked up the first ball and threw it...and missed. Nicole turned away. She couldn't watch anymore. She took out her cell phone and considered sending someone a text message, but she only knew a few people who were using them regularly. They cost $.10 each. She opted for solitaire instead.

"Haaaaaaaaaaaa!!!" Marcus belted out his excitement just at that moment. "Told ya, baby girl! Told ya I'd get win it! Pick which one you want."

"Oh goodness, I don't need one of those," she said, waving him off with a smile.

"Come on, pick one. What about the purple one? I know that's your favorite color. Hey man, give me that purple bear on the third shelf. Yeah...yeah that one right there," he instructed. The teen handed him the bear and he turned and held it out to Nicole. She folded her arms and shook her head.

"Marcus, I don't need that silly bear!"

"You sure? Let's name him."

"How do you know it's a 'him'?"

Marcus held the bear's sewn on mouth to his ear and pretended to be listening to the bear tell him something. He smiled and laughed as if they were having a real conversation.

"Well, Jamaal here tells me that he knows he is a boy because he can't wait to be held by you and drawn in close to those soft, round tittayssss," he said, laughing. *"Yes, his name is Jamaal, and yes, he said 'tittaysssss' just like that."*

Nicole laughed out loud. Marcus always had a way of making her laugh, even when she was frustrated or mad at him. She moved towards him and took the bear from him. He pulled her into a hug and lifted her up off of her feet, causing her to yelp. He buried his lips into her neck and twirled her around.

"Put me down, Sir!!" she yelled while laughing and halfheartedly pounding his chest. He kept twirling her as if she were as light as cotton.

"Never!"

"Never?"

"Never, baby girl."

"Promise?"

"Absolutely!"

"Hmmm. We'll see about that," Nicole said, not quite doubting, but not quite believing his promise of forever. Things were so up and down for them and were becoming increasingly tense. This evening was a nice reprieve and she loved this side of him. He was so playful, warm, and considerate. He made her feel special and, well... Jamaal.

"You're crushing Jamaal," she informed him.

"Oh, oh, my bad. Can't crush our boy," he said as he backed up.

"Our boy? I thought he was mine?"

"True, true, but...someday we're going to have our own little Jamaal, and maybe a Jamilah."

"You want to have children with me, Sir?"

"Yes of course, I do. Why wouldn't I?"

"I just wasn't sure that was something you'd even thought about in passing, much less given deeper consideration."

"I just said I'm never letting you go, woman. Why wouldn't I put some babies in you?" Marcus laughed as he swatted her backside. "Those hips were made for carrying my strong, bigheaded babies."

"Whatever..."

"You gonna have my babies?"

"Marcus..."

"You've been using my given name a lot more lately. What's up with that??" Marcus's brows furrowed a bit with genuine concern.

"Nothing... Sir, it's nothing. Sure. I'll carry your bigheaded babies," she said with a smile, redirecting the conversation. A state fair was not the place to have what could be a passionately embarrassing discussion. "I don't know about those names though. Jamilah is nice, but Jamaal? I don't think so," she said shaking her head.

"Oh, I was only joking about that. Definitely Marcus, Jr." he said, flashing the smile that always made Nicole's knees buckle. Today was no different. She stared into his eyes, making clear her intention and desire. Marcus picked up on it.

"Nasty girl. Tsk tsk tsk."

"Ha ha. Whatever. You love it."

Marcus paused. He cupped her face in his large hands and leaned in close as if to kiss her. He closed his eyes and inhaled deeply.

"I know most of the time, I ain't worth half the time you give me. But... shit. I love you. I do. I

love you and I need you, and that's why I'm never letting you go."

Nicole kissed his lips gently, then again, more deeply.

"Promise?"

"Mmmhmm," he moaned into her lips. "Now come on, let's go home so I can give you what you want. My baby girl is so fucking nasty, I love it!" He grabbed her empty hand and led her towards the parking lot so they could go home and he could lay her out. Nicole let out a deep breath when they arrived at their car.

They each got in on their respective sides and after fastening their seat belts, Nicole turned to Marcus.

"I love you, too. And I'm not going anywhere, Sir. I promise."

Marcus smiled, accepting her pledge.

****

"You think you know so much so you should know she promised she would be with me forever. She said...she would never...ever...leave me," Marcus bit out, his breathing becoming more rugged. "Remember that, baby girl? Remember when you promised me? I promised you, too, and I don't go back on my promises...like you do."

Marcus released Nicole and she fell to the ground gasping for air. David instinctively moved towards her, but Marcus quickly moved in between them, moving the gun to David's cheek, close to His nose.

"Don't... you... fucking... move," he warned slowly, clearly, making sure David understood the brevity of their predicament. "You took her from me. You took everything. Everything I had, I had with her..."

"You lost her."

"You *stole* her."

"She left before I arrived."

"It's over Marcus!" Nicole called out from her position on the floor. "Do you remember what you did to me? Huh?? Do you want to see the scar?" She scooted back against the wall, massaging her neck as bruises began to surface. "It's over..." she whispered.

Marcus shifted in his stance. His pistol-wielding hand began to tremble from holding his arm up as long as it had been.

"She left of her own free will because you damned near destroyed her. Accept it. You lost out on an amazing woman because... you are a punk-assed piece of shit!!"

With that declaration, David ducked His head, sidestepped Marcus's aim and punched him in the appendix region. Startled, Marcus squeezed off a shot. The bullet shot through the window behind the recliner in the living room. He doubled over, caught off-guard by the punch to his abdomen, and staggered back a bit. David punched him again, this time on the other side of Marcus' core. David was shorter than Marcus, but He did not let that intimidate Him. He tried to force the gun out of Marcus' hand, but Marcus came back with some blows of his own. The two men fell to the ground and were scuffling, going back and forth, and exchanging places atop of the other.

Nicole screamed for help, hoping any of her neighbors were still home and could hear them.

Someone had to have heard the gunshot, right? Nicole thought to herself and she scrambled to her feet and quickly scanned the room for something she could use to help David overtake Marcus.

"Stop this!! Marcus, stop this!!! This is fucking crazy!!!" she screamed, frantic, terrified. She ran to the hallway to see if anyone had come out of their apartments, but it was deserted. She ran back in and grabbed her purse, seeking her cell phone. She was going to call the police. She found it and began dialing 9-1-*POW!!!*

Another shot rang out and the scuffling stopped. Nicole dropped her phone and fell to her knees.

"You shot... Oh my God... oh my God... oh my God...y-y-ou shot..oh Godddd!!"

Marcela dug her small hands into the dirt, chasing the pink earthworm that caught her attention as her parents hovered over her and spoke in hushed tones. She twisted her index finger and thumb into the ground, trying her best to grab the slimy, slithering worm. It got away from her and the tears began to form in her eyes. She rubbed a dirty fist in her eye and began to wail as the soil got into her right eye and began to burn.

"Mamaaaaaa" she wailed emphatically. She reached for her mother's healing embrace.

"Oh baby, what happened?" Nicole asked her five-year-old daughter as she reached down to lift her up into her arms.

"Mama...mama!!" Marcela continued to cry out.

"Shhhh. It's OK, my love. It's gonna be alright, my baby," Nicole reassured her, swaying her body side-to-side as she held her daughter close to her heart. "You just have a little bit of dirt. Let mama see," she said as she reached her hand towards the child's eye. Marcela shook her head furiously and pulled back away, pushing her hands into her mother's chest as she tried to get away.

"Come to Daddy," her father cooed, extending his arms out to her. Marcela smiled through her tears and gladly reached out to her father, preferring his hugs to her mother's eye blowing. He grabbed her under her arms and pulled her close to his chest.

"Now, Marcy, you have to let Daddy get the dirt out. Hold still," he softly commanded. He reached his hand towards her eye, spread the lids and quickly blew into her eye repeatedly. She batted her eyelashes a few times and the flecks of dirt came out with the tears. After receiving her father's tender care for a few seconds, she seemed to be feeling better.

"There, there... alllll better," her father confirmed, bouncing her up and down on. He pulled her close again, and breathed in her thick, soft hair which was fastened into a neat bun atop her head. She had a few stray tendrils along the crown, one of which he wrapped around his finger.

"It's so good to see you, baby girl. I missed you so much this time."

"I missed you, too, Daddy!"

Nicole stood quietly, observing the exchange between father and daughter. He had just returned from a business trip and as Marcela grew older, she struggled more with her father leaving on his trips. Nicole knew that Marcela did not quite understand why Daddy would be gone for such long stretches, but when he returned, she would be enveloped by the enormity of his love and tenderness. Marcela was truly a Daddy's Girl, and she relished every moment her father spent doting on her.

Nicole watched them snuggle and cast her gaze downward, slightly beyond where they stood. She focused the small marble tombstone by her husband's foot, quietly reflecting on what brought them there at that moment. The engraved words were simple:

BELOVED SON AND BROTHER.

It had been six years, to the day, since Marcus showed up at her apartment, enraged and out of his mind, and confronted David with a gun. She had returned to her apartment because she wanted to tell David about the strange man she encountered outside in the parking lot. Since He did not answer His phone, she went back to the apartment to make sure everything was OK. When she walked in, she was nearly paralyzed by the scene before her—Marcus stood before David, gun pointed at His chest, seemingly out-of-touch with the reality and brevity of the situation.

Marcus was hurting and demanding that Nicole return to him and be with him, despite her decision to stay with the love of her life, David. David remained steadfast and attempted to rationalize with Marcus, but His efforts were futile as Marcus was not trying to hear anything other than Nicole's agreement to be with him. Nicole's entrance was just the slight distraction David needed to attempt to physically subdue Marcus, so he took a chance. The two men scuffled as David tried to separate Marcus from his gun. In the scuffle, the gun fired and Marcus was fatally struck in the chest.

Marcus rolled over onto the ground and David scrambled to His feet and rushed to Nicole. Nicole screamed and then tried to tell David to help Marcus, but she couldn't get all of the words out. She felt herself struggling to breathe and looked around at the spinning room. Everything went black...

When she came to, Nicole was inside of an ambulance being poked and prodded by a female EMS worker. David was nowhere to be found. She became frantic and demanded to know where He was. The EMS worker tried to calm her down by telling her that she needed to relax, but Nicole was not interested in relaxing—she needed to know where her man was. The woman told Nicole that David remained in the apartment and was speaking with police officers.

"He didn't do it!!" Nicole yelled. "He didn't do anything! It was Marcus! Marcus tried to kill us!" she continued yelling, her voice hoarse and breaking. She began to cry and tried to sit up, but as she shot up too quickly, she felt woozy and fell back onto the stretcher. *Oh God,* she thought, *Please don't let them take Him away. He didn't do it. He didn't do it...*

Nicole blinked a few times and came back to the present. David and Marcela were now standing side-by-side at the tombstone. David was more solemn, now, and Marcela was fidgety, but seemed to understand her Daddy's change in mood.

"Baby, we have something important to tell you," He began. He took a few deep breaths and grabbed His daughter's hand more tightly. He crouched down, resting on His heels as He looked into her eyes. "Marcus, the man who is buried here, was the man who created you, baby girl," David said, simply.

David and Nicole agreed to bring Marcela there because she was old enough to learn the truth. While they knew she would not fully comprehend what it meant, they agreed it was time for her to learn the truth. In the short time that Nicole experienced amnesia after her fall, she believed that she and Marcus were in love and a couple. She spent time with Marcus and was intimate with him, not knowing that their relationship had long been over. Marcus took advantage of her lapse in memory and welcomed the opportunity to sleep with her again while she seemed willing to engage in sexual activity with him. Though she could feel something was off, she did not completely trust her own mind, so she did what she believed was normal for them.

After she regained her memory and realized that she belonged with David, she was overcome with regret and betrayal—Marcus manipulated her into having sex with her. He knew she would not consent to sex if she was not experiencing trauma-induced amnesia, and for a long time, Nicole struggled with what he had done to her. She opened up to David about it, right after they had physically reconnected, and He understood. While disgusted by Marcus's manipulation, not once did He blame her or show any kind of anger or resentment towards her. His anger and hatred of Marcus only grew, so when Marcus appeared in their home, David was ready to handle Marcus, man-to-man.

He did not, however, plan to shoot and kill him.

David went with police to the precinct, but was not arrested. He cooperated with the police, explaining how shooting Marcus was an accident and how His own actions were in response to threats to His and Nicole's lives. Nicole corroborated His story, as did one of their neighbors who spoke to police on the scene, and the cameras in and around their apartment complex. It became clear to investigators that the shooting was truly an act of self-defense, so no charges were filed against David. Marcus' death was his own doing, even if David was the one who pulled the trigger.

"Marcus and Mama made you together, but Marcus died before you were born," David continued. "I have loved Mommy for as long as I can remember and I knew, then, that I would love you, too... with everything that I have. I knew, before you were born, that you were sent here for me and Mommy to love and adore."

"Mama told me that a man puts his penis in a woman's vagina and that's how people make babies sometimes," Marcela replied. "Did Marcus put his penis in Mama's vagina?"

Nicole could not help but chuckle at her daughter's precociousness. David looked up at her, eyebrow raised, and the twinkle in His eye betrayed the frown He wore. He looked back at His daughter.

"Is that what Mommy told you?" He asked.

"Yup!"

"Well, your mama was right and yes, that's what happened."

"You put your penis in mama's vagina, too, right?" she asked, pointing at Nicole's bulging belly. She was just over 6-months pregnant with their son. Nicole laughed heartily at that question. Marcela went still for a moment, looked down at her shoes, and she kicked the ground a bit.

"Is Marcus my real Daddy?" she asked her parents.

"Daddy is your real Daddy, Marcy," Nicole replied immediately. She walked over to be closer to the two most important people in her life. She leaned forward to caress Marcela's face, lifting her chin up so she could meet her gaze. "Baby, Marcus was not a good man. He hurt Mama and tried to hurt Daddy. We wanted you to know the truth and we will tell you more when you're older. Just know this—your Daddy loves you with everything He is. In the eyes of the law and in the hearts of this family, Daddy is your *real* Daddy, OK?"

Marcela looked up at her mother's reassuring smile, then looked up at her Daddy, who was rubbing Nicole's back. She looked between the two of them a few times and then broke into a smile. She threw herself into a wide hug, trying to grab both of them in her small arms. The family shared a big hug and right at that moment, Nicole's stomach began to move, eliciting an excited yelp from Marcela.

"He moved! He moved! I felt him!" she yelled, clapping her hands with glee. Nicole clutched her stomach, feeling another of the mild contractions she had been feeling for the past few hours. She experienced the same when carrying Marcela, so she was not at all worried.

David wrapped His arms around Nicole from behind and rubbed her belly, feeling His son make his presence known. He nuzzled her neck and whispered, "I adore you, Star."

"And I, you, Sir," she replied.

"You saved me."

"You gave me life."

"You are giving me life, again."

"I'm honored to carry your child, Sir."

"We've been through so much, Star. Too much…"

"I know."

"We can begin a new chapter when he arrives."

"Yes…"

"Thank you for loving me."

"Thank you for making me your wife."

"She's so beautiful… your twin."

"She has his eyes…"

"She has your spirit."

"She is her Daddy's child."

David took a deep breath, inhaling Nicole's scent, a mix of Egyptian Musk oil and impending new motherhood. He looked down at His son's limbs poking at the walls around him. He looked up at His daughter who was back on her knees chasing another Earthworm. He looked up to the sky and sighed deeply.

"Mine."

Nicole leaned her head back against His shoulder and followed His gaze towards the sky. She too, sighed deeply.

"Always."

Nicole felt another contraction, but it was a much stronger pain this time. She doubled over forward and David caught her.

"Star, you OK? Is it the baby?"

Nicole nodded as she tried to catch her breath. She continued to breathe and stood upright. David did His best to stabilize her and support her posture. "Come on, let's go. Marcy!" He called, "Come on, baby girl. Time to go home!"

Marcy made her way towards them as David guided Nicole towards their car. She was oblivious to what was going on with her mother, which was probably for the best. When they reached the car, David opened the door and helped His wife sit down. As she slid down, she cried out as another pain coursed through her body. The tears came to her eyes and she moaned, "Not my baby... please, not my baby..."

****

Nicole became acutely aware of her breathing because she felt a cool breeze flowing into her nose. Before she opened her eyes, she thought that it was odd that the air seemed so crisp and fresh. She tried opening her eyes, but her eyelids felt heavy. She heard a steady beeping and several voices around her. She recognized two of the men's voices, but not the woman who was speaking to them. The men sounded intense, maybe they were arguing, she could not really tell.

She then became aware of the pounding in her head. It was a headache unlike anything she had ever experienced before. She opened her lips to tell everyone to be quiet, maybe ask for pain killers.

"Why the fuck are you in here? Today of all days?" One of the men was questioning the other. "How many times do I have to tell you to stay far away from Nicole as possible?? Huh?? It's been over seven weeks already and you're *still* not welcomed here!"

"Look, man," Marcus began, "I just wanted to come by and check on her, OK?" Marcus stood still, annoyed that David interrupted his singing. "It's Valentine's Day, man, have a heart."

Sir...

Her eyes opened and she looked toward the sound of His voice. She saw Him facing off with Marcus. *Why is Marcus here?* She was confused, her head was pounding, and she was beginning to get a sense of her surroundings.

She was in a hospital.

"The baby!!! Sir, where's our baby? Where's our son??" she screamed, frantically grabbing at her flat stomach as she looked around the room for a sign of her child. David rushed over to her and grabbed her into His arms.

"Oh Star, oh baby, you're OK... you're OK... oh my love, my heart..." He cooed as He tried to soothe her. He stroked her hair, wiping away the sweat beads forming along her temples. He was so relieved that she was awake, that He ignored everyone else in the room also interested in her regaining consciousness.

"Everything is going to be OK, Star. I promise, I will never let anything else happen to you again," He continued, assuring her that she was safe with Him as His grip tightened. Nicole pushed back as she tried to disentangle herself from his embrace.

"Where's Marcy??" she demanded.

"B-baby... w-w-what are you talking about? Who is...Marcy?"

"What the hell do you mean, 'Who is Marcy?'? What's wrong with you? Where's our daughter? Where's my baby, David?? What happened to our son??"

Nicole became frantic and started pulling at the wires that were hooked up to her. The nurse called for assistance and rushed over to help David calm her down.

"Yo, she's wilding," murmured Marcus, as he backed away from the bed and moved towards the far corner of the room.

"Where's my baby? What happened to my baby?" she continued to ask, crying and pleading for an answer from David, the nurse, anyone. Three more hospital personnel entered the room and two approached the bed.

"Please back away, sir," one of the nurses instructed.

"No! She is my fiancée," He asserted. "I'm not going anywhere. She needs me. She keeps talking about children. We don't have children. Something's wrong!"

"Sir, please give us space," another nurse requested again. David reluctantly backed up a couple of feet. Nicole reached out to Him.

"No!!! Sir, don't leave me!! Don't leave me again!!" she yelled. David rushed back to her side, pushing one of the nurses out of the way.

"I'll never leave you, Star. Never. I'm here. I'm here," He promised.

Nicole began to calm down, but she was still crying as she rubbed her stomach. She shook her head back-and-forth, fearing the absolute worst—she lost their baby.

"What happened? Did I lose the baby?"

David looked at her quizzically. He looked at the nurse. "What is she talking about? Nurse, is she... is she pregnant?" W-was she pregnant?"

The first nurse looked at Him with something odd in her eyes. "Let's talk outside," she said, motioning for Him to join her outside of the room. He squeezed Nicole's shoulder and promised He would return. When He stepped outside, the nurse took a deep breath and began to give Him the news.

"As you know, your fiancée experienced serious head trauma during her fall. We ran several tests to get a better idea of any internal injuries. We conducted a routine pregnancy test, too," she started. "Were you aware that she is pregnant?"

"Pregnant?" He asked again. "How is that possible? She's been on birth control for at least two years."

"We ran the test twice," the nurse said confidently. "She is definitely pregnant, and based on the sonogram, measurements, and presence of a heartbeat, she's about 7or 8 weeks along." David was stunned. He could not help but look at the nurse with complete confusion.

"That doesn't make any sense. Why didn't she tell me?" He looked back at the room and saw that Nicole was calmer now, but was still rubbing her stomach.

"I'm not sure, but I'm not entirely certain she was aware herself."

"But she just asked about our baby..."

"I don't know... Sometimes, when people suffer head trauma such as she has, they experience different types of amnesia or other cognitive impairments. She might just be a bit confused. Why don't I get the doctor to come in and talk with you? Maybe she will have more answers," she suggested, trying to offer some form of consolation to David.

David went back into the room and to Nicole's bedside. He looked over at Marcus, met his eyes, and motioned for him to leave the room. Marcus did not put up a fight this time and he quietly exited the hospital room where Nicole had been in care for several weeks. David stroked her temples and grabbed her hand. He was overwhelmed by everything that had just happened in the past ten minutes that he was shaking. He tried to calm His body, His mind, His heart.

"Star, baby...?"

"What's happening to me, Sir?"

"You took a really nasty fall, baby. You...fell... and you hit your head pretty hard," He began. "You have been in a coma for several weeks. It is Valentine's Day. You're in the hospital. I've been here every day, waiting for you to come back to me..."

Nicole closed her eyes and tears began to course down her cheeks, burning the truth of what He was saying into her skin. There was no Marcy. There was no... baby.

"Don't cry, Star. Please. I can't bear it. You're awake. I've prayed every single day for this and now, to know you're pregnant—"

"What did you say?"

"Baby, the nurse just told me that you're pregnant with our child," David said, smiling down at her. He was still in shock at the revelation Himself, but He could feel the joy beginning to spread within Him. "I'm going to be a father!"

"It was so real," Nicole began. "You shot Marcus.. and Marcy was his and..."

"Shhhh baby. It's OK. It's all over now. You're here now, with me. We're together. We're going to get married. We're going to keep our baby safe," David promised.

He leaned down and kissed Nicole on her stomach. As He stood up, the doctor entered the hospital room and He began asking her questions about

Nicole's condition and the things she said. Nicole lay in the bed, listening intently, but the pounding in her head began to lessen, so she found herself drifting back to sleep.

After a few moments, the doctor left and David returned to Nicole's bedside. He traced His thumb along her lips with His left hand and with His right, He covered her womb.

Mine.

Made in the USA
Middletown, DE
30 September 2015